D0126755

KILLING A STRANGER

KILLING A STRANGER

Jane A. Adams

This first world edition published in Great Britain 2006 by
SEVERN HOUSE PUBLISHERS LTD of
9–15 High Street, Sutton, Surrey SM1 1DF.
This first world edition published in the USA 2006 by
SEVERN HOUSE PUBLISHERS INC of
595 Madison Avenue, New York, N.Y. 10022.

British Library Cataloguing in Publication Data

Adams,   Jane,   1950-
    Killing a stranger. - (A Naomi Blake mystery)
    1.   Ex-police officers - Fiction
    2.   Detective and mystery stories
    I.   Title
    823.9'14 [F]

    ISBN-13: 978-0-7278-6357 -7
    ISBN-10: 0-7278-6357-6

Typeset by Palimpsest Book Production Ltd.,
Polmont, Stirlingshire, Scotland.
Printed and bound in Great Britain by
MPG Books Ltd., Bodmin, Cornwall.

Many thanks to Catherine and Rob Davies (www.echurch-uk.org) for their information and support. Bless you both.

Prologue

He was covered in blood, his hands, his face, the open jacket and white T-shirt beneath.

'Mum!'

He staggered in through the open door and fell in a heap on the hall floor.

'Mum, he's dead. I killed him.'

Clara couldn't absorb the words; they were too alien, too meaningless. 'You're hurt,' she said. 'Oh, Rob, Oh God, what have you done?'

She knelt beside him, pulling him into her arms, her hands moving over his body as she sought the wound that was producing so much blood.

'It isn't me,' he whispered. 'Mum, I killed him. He's lying there, dead, and I did it.' He turned to look at her, his face grey with shock, eyes stricken, filled with such horror that Clara could hardly bear to look into them.

'Rob? Rob, darling, what are you talking about? You're hurt, Rob, let me help you.'

Even as she spoke the words, Clara was aware of how inadequate they sounded. She still couldn't comprehend what was happening, but her brain was telling her that this was bigger, more terrible than anything she had ever imagined could happen to her son, and her stomach tightened, gut writhing in fear.

Somehow, she helped him to his feet and they staggered together into the kitchen. Clara pulled a chair out from the table and sat him down. Again, she moved her hands across his body, searching for the wound. Rob being hurt, even

1

badly hurt, was easier to think about than that other thing. That thing he kept telling her.

'Mum. . .' More of a wail now, despairing, horrified. 'I'm scared, Mum.' A child's cry, a child waking from a nightmare and finding that it hadn't gone away.

'It's all right,' she told him. 'It's all right, whatever it is, we can work it out.'

What should she do? She pulled him close to her and stroked his hair. Her hands came away red and sticky and she couldn't hold back the little whimper of horror.

He jerked his head back and looked up at her. She could see the hurt in his eyes, that little cry of disgust and horror, he interpreted as disgust with him. Horror at what he had done.

'Rob, no, no, it will be all right.' She reached for him again, thinking, once more how inadequate the words were in the face of such anguish, such pain. But words were all she had and she knew that something had to be done. 'Rob, we've got to . . .'

Got to what? Making tea, finding biscuits, the usual recourse in times of upset didn't quite cut it this time. Stiff drink? She had some whisky in the cupboard, stored, ready for Christmas. Should she get it?

'You've got to phone the police,' Rob whispered. 'Mum, I killed a man.'

Gently, almost as though he were now that adult, he pushed her away from him and pointed towards the hall. 'Phone them, Mum, please. I can't. I don't know what to say.'

'Rob?' Clara could feel the tears pricking her eyes, then, next moment, trickling uncontrolled down her cheeks. She brushed them aside, then nodded mutely and backed away from him through the kitchen door and out into the hall.

She wasn't sure how she kept her hand steady enough to dial or her voice even enough to reply to the operator. 'Police,' she asked. Police and ambulance, still clinging to the faint hope that it was Rob's blood.

'He says he's killed someone,' she whispered. 'He says . . . and oh, God, there's so much blood.'

She caught sight of herself in the hall mirror. Tears still

2

flooded her eyes and poured down her cheeks, tears running rivulets through smears of red. She dropped the phone, raised her hands again to brush the tears away, to wipe the stains from her face, but the blood was on her hands and she only spread it further, smeared it across her cheeks and temples. Her eyes.

'Oh, Rob!'

The operators voice, dim, but insistent sounded from the phone but Clara didn't hear. She swung from the mirror as she heard the back door slam. Running through to the kitchen, she was in time to see him stumbling through the garden gate.

'Rob!'

But he was gone. She stood at the gate peering through the gloom, listening to the sound of his footsteps as he ran away from her and knew she'd never catch him now.

The police found her crouching by the garden gate, shaking and weeping and calling her son's name, her face and hands still smeared with blood.

One

'I saw the police car and the ambulance and they took Rob's mum away and then I left. I didn't know what to do.'

Becky's face crumpled with distress. Charlie was scuffing his feet against the mud and gravel of the towpath, his hands thrust deep in his pockets and his back half turned to them. Patrick recognised the body language of extreme discomfort and knew he'd get no help from that direction.

He managed to ask, 'You said you went back this morning?'

Becky, who had already reprised her story several times, nodded emphatically. 'I knocked at the door and then went round the back. The gate was open; Clara never leaves the gate open. I went and looked through the window and, like I told you, there was this policeman in the kitchen and this guy in a white overall, like you see them on the telly.'

Patrick nodded. 'SOCO,' he said. 'Scenes of Crime Officer.'

'I know who it was. I watch CSI, don't I?'

Charlie laughed. 'They don't wear white overalls on CSI, they go around in their posh clothes contaminating the crime scene. Isn't that right, Patrick?'

Charlie was hiding behind the incidental again, just like he had all morning. Patrick just nodded. 'Where the hell did Rob get to?' he fumed. 'I mean . . .'

Becky hunched her shoulders deeper into her coat and shivered. 'It's cold,' she said. 'They didn't take Rob away, just Clara.'

She got up, angry with herself. 'I should have asked them, should have gone up and told them I was looking for my

5

boyfriend and that they were taking his mam away. I should have gone up to Clara and talked to her.' She bit her lip hard enough to blanch it where her teeth pressed down. Patrick could see the tears about to start again.

'Mum and . . . *Him* . . .' *Him* Patrick knew, was her step-father.

'Mum and Him, they said I should keep out of it and if the police came round I was to say nothing. Just to tell them Rob was at the party and then he left and I don't know where he went.'

Charlie's laugh was harsher this time. 'Well, you *don't* bloody know, do you? I mean, none of us bloody do.'

Patrick sighed and got up from his cold seat on the iron bench. He slid an arm round Becky's shoulder. They'd been good friends now for almost a year and he felt that a brotherly arm was ok. She seemed to think so too because she laid her head against his shoulder and swore softly at the unfathomable pain of it all.

Patrick towered over her now, while only six months or so ago he had been eye level. He was still skinny as a lath though, attempting to disguise the fact with baggy shirts and skater jeans and, lately, a long leather coat that had been an early Christmas present from his mother and step-father in America.

Patrick liked his step-father and his stepbrothers. It would never have occurred to him to think of Ray as *Him*. He spoke to his mother once a week and the new husband and surrogate brothers always joined the conversation on the speakerphone they had set up in the living room of the large bungalow they owned a few hundred yards from the beach.

It was a striking contrast to the tiny little house – two up, two down, kitchen and bathroom tagged on the back – which he shared with his dad. His dad, Harry, had been a bit put out with the gift of the coat, but, as Patrick said to him, 'Mum and Ray can *only* buy me things. I'm not there, am I?' He thought his dad had understood. The coat was too cool to send back anyway.

'Will the police still be there?' Charlie asked.

Patrick glanced at Charlie and shrugged. 'I don't know,' he said.

'You must have some idea. I mean . . .'

Patrick knew what he meant. His friend, Naomi was an ex-policewoman and her boyfriend was a Detective Inspector. 'It would depend what went on,' he said. 'If they've got SOCO in . . .'

If SOCO were there, then something bad had happened. Something that needed a fingerprint officer, forensics, samples taken . . . samples of what?

'Not good, then,' Charlie was just confirming what they had all been thinking. 'Fuck, Rob, what the hell have you done?'

'Rob wouldn't do nothing,' Becky defended. She pulled away from Patrick and flopped back down on the bench, head bent, shoulders shaking.

'I didn't mean . . .' Charlie threw his hands in the air and turned his back once again. Patrick could see him clenching and unclenching his jaw. You couldn't cry when you were male and just turned eighteen, but Patrick could see it was costing him to keep up that pretence. Charlie and Rob had been friends for years, for long before Patrick had come on the scene; Charlie was thinking the worst.

Patrick glanced along the towpath. Rain clouds gathered down by the marina, behind the burnt out factory building scheduled for demolition, cranes already in place. Patrick had been trapped in that building the day it caught fire. Hard to believe it was more than two years before. It had taken them a long time, he thought, to figure they should pull the rest down.

The day was bleak and grey and moisture chilled the air even before the threatened rain began. His feet were frozen in his boots and his hands, never good with the cold, were numb at the fingertips and turning blue.

'Come on,' he said, gesturing to the other two and striding off towards the steps that led back on to the road.

'Come on where?'

'Naomi. We're going to see Naomi. She might be able to find something out. Ask Alec.'

'You think she can?' Becky's voice was thick with tears.

Patrick shrugged. He didn't know. If she could, she

probably would, but he'd been round Naomi and Alec for long enough to be familiar with the idea of operational integrity; they might well not be able to tell him anything that wasn't already in the public domain. 'Don't know,' he admitted, 'but you got any better ideas? It's too cold to hang about here anyway. It's either that or back to Rob's place.'

He halted, waiting for a decision. Rob's house was in the other direction.

Charlie shook his head. 'No,' he said, 'if Clara wasn't there an hour ago and the police *were* . . .' It was unlikely she'd be back there now.

'Ok, Naomi's it is then.' Decision made, Patrick walked fast, the others scurrying to catch him and then keeping pace with the same sense of urgency. He could hear Becky sobbing still, trying not to, but the odd sniff and gulp giving her away. He reached out a hand and took hers, conscious of how warm her hand was in his cold one. She squeezed his fingers gratefully and then let go. Patrick angrily pushed the thought away that, in any case, Rob wasn't good enough for her.

Where the hell was Rob? And wherever he was, was he all right?

Naomi opened the door and stood aside. 'How many of you are there?' she asked. 'Oh, and Patrick, your dad phoned, thought you might turn up here. He said to tell you he'll be home about two.'

'OK, thanks,' Patrick mumbled. 'There's me and Charlie, you've met Charlie?'

'Um, yes. Hi Charlie.'

'And this is Becky.'

'Hi, Becky, come along in. You want some coffee?'

'Thanks,' Patrick said.

Naomi heard him go past her and slide the heavy coat from his shoulders before dropping on to the blue sofa beneath the window; his favourite spot in her flat. The others moved more uncertainly, hovering a bit before Naomi told them to make themselves at home. 'You take sugar?'

'Um, one please,' the girl called Becky told her.

8

She's been crying, Naomi thought. Either that, or she had the mother of all colds. 'Should I come and help you . . .?' Becky offered.

Naomi smiled in her direction. She was used to people being disconcerted by her blindness and assuming she might not be able to manage on her own and she had long ago given up taking offence. 'I'm fine,' she said. 'But thanks anyway. Say hi to Napoleon.' She added. 'Don't let Patrick get all the fuss.'

Becky laughed uncertainly but Naomi heard her go over to where Patrick was sitting and the steady thump thump of the dog's heavy tail against the wooden floor as he realized he was about to get twice the attention.

What was going on, Naomi wondered as she went through to her little kitchen and started to make the coffee. It was always a pleasure to have Patrick visit and he was a frequent occupant of the blue sofa, but, she sensed, this was different. She could tell, without needing to see their faces, that this trio felt the weight of the world on their shoulders.

The story had taken a while to tell, Naomi coaxing it out of them at first, then, as they became more confident of her willingness to listen without judgement, they talked over one another in their hurry to get the story out and Naomi had to slow them down, go back over some details to make sure she had it right.

'So,' she said slowly. 'Charlie's eighteenth birthday party and everything seems fine, except Rob had something on his mind for days that he wouldn't talk about.'

'Weeks, more like,' Charlie interrupted.

Naomi held up a hand to pause before he went off on that tangent again. 'OK, we'll get back to that. Let's get the time-line sorted first. You all agree it was just after ten when Rob left the party?'

She felt the pause as they all looked at one another.

'Yeah,' Charlie said. 'It was only just after ten. My dad and my uncle decided it was time for speeches.' Naomi could hear the embarrassment in his voice as he remembered. 'They were pissed.'

9

'Part of parental duties,' Naomi told him. 'Embarrassing your kids.'

She heard Patrick laugh.

'Yeah, right,' Charlie said. 'Anyway, I got dragged back into the quiet room and someone told the band to stop playing for a bit. Patrick was with me but I looked round for Rob and I saw him by the exit door, with Becks. He went out and Becky followed him. I wondered what was going on, but Dad and Uncle Tim were well into it by then and by the time they'd done making their speeches and stuff, Becks was back. That was about half ten and we reckon they must have started up not later than about ten past.'

'You've talked about this a lot, obviously.'

'Rob stormed off down the street,' Becky took up the story from her perspective. 'I shouted after him to come back or at least wait up for me. He just told me to go back inside. I thought about going home, but it was too early and I knew Mum and *Him* would want to know what was up and they're down on Rob anyway, don't like me seeing him.'

'*Him*,' Naomi enquired, noting the emphasis.

'My so called step-father. Like he's got any right to criticize.'

Naomi decided to let that can of worms remain unopened for the moment. She asked, 'So, when did you eventually leave the party?'

'It was about eleven fifteen, eleven thirty, something like that. I decided to walk to Rob's place, have it out with him, tell him if he didn't stop fu . . . messing me around, that was it. Finished. I got to his house a bit after twelve and the police were there and the ambulance.'

'No sign of Rob?'

She sensed the girl shake her head, then remember that Naomi couldn't see. 'No, nothing,' she said. 'And when I went back this morning, the police were still in the house, at least, one of them was and the SOCO woman in the back room.'

'What do you think might have happened?' Patrick's voice shook slightly. He coughed to cover up.

Naomi thought about it. 'Have you spoken to anyone? Parents?'

Of course they hadn't, she thought, at least not in any detail.

'My mam wanted to know where I'd been. I didn't get home 'til half one and I was supposed to come back in a taxi at half twelve. I told her . . . sort of.'

'You told her you'd gone to the house?'

'And they told me to say nothing if the police asked. Not to get involved. *He* said it was none of my business, but Rob's my boyfriend, so of course it is.'

'If the police do ask you anything,' Naomi cautioned, 'you've got to tell them all you can remember. If you don't, you could end up in deeper trouble than any your parents can hand out.'

She left that to sink in while she made more coffee. Patrick wandered into the kitchen behind her and half closed the door. 'Nomi, it's bad, isn't it?'

'It doesn't sound good. There's been nothing on the news?'

'No, we listened on the local radio.'

'So, it's unlikely to have been a fire, car accident, anything like that. Patrick, did you know Rob well, I've heard you talk about him, but . . .'

'Pretty well. We'd only really been friends this year.'

'Could he have got into a fight?'

He was close enough in the tiny kitchen for her to feel him shrug. 'Maybe, he has a bit of a temper, he gets frustrated and impatient with stuff, but it's all over in a flash. He never goes looking for trouble. Naomi, we've texted everyone we know, no one's seen him since last night.'

Texted, she thought, not phoned or spoken to. It was an interesting generational shift.

'Here,' he said. 'Give me the tray and then you can bring the biscuit tin.'

'Have you thought to call the hospitals?' Naomi asked as they settled down again.

'Hospitals? You think Rob might be hurt?' They'd all thought of this, Naomi guessed, but Becky sounded horrified at it being spoken aloud.

'I'm thinking,' Naomi said calmly, 'that if Rob's mum was taken to hospital, he might be there with her.'

11

'How would he know?'

'If he turned up at home, the police would have told him. It sounds as though there's been an officer there overnight. Clara might have been hurt, maybe, worst case scenario, there was a break-in and she interrupted them. That would explain the SOCO.'

'Right,' Patrick said. She could feel the relief. Focused so much on their friend, they hadn't thought that he might be the secondary character in the drama.

'I mean, that would still be terrible,' Patrick added. 'But . . . Naomi, can you call them?'

'Get me the phone book and read out the numbers,' she said. 'Let's see what we can find out.

They struck lucky on the second call. Mrs Clara Beresford was an in-patient, brought in late last night, but they could release no further details. Was Naomi Blake a relative?

Naomi considered lying, but she had already guessed there might be an officer on watch in the hospital and they would like as not recognize her name.

'Is her son with her?' Naomi asked.

'No,' she was told. There had been no sign of her son.

Naomi replaced the receiver, aware of the expectant hush. 'Clara was admitted last night,' she said. 'But I'm sorry, there's no sign of Rob.'

The disappointment was palpable and she felt bad about having let them down after building their hopes.

'You said he's seemed worried about something for the past few weeks. Any idea what?'

'No,' Becky replied so quickly Naomi knew they'd already covered that ground over and over. 'I kept on at him to tell me, we all did.'

'He let something slip,' Charlie added slowly and Naomi knew she was now being trusted with information the other adults in their lives wouldn't be getting. 'He said he was looking for his dad and he didn't want his mum finding out in case she got upset. He said he'd found a letter or something.'

'His dad,' Naomi prompted. She could feel the collective closing of ranks and knew she'd get little more from them until they'd had a chance to talk it through.

12

'His mum brought him up on her own,' Becky told her. 'She's nice,' she added unexpectedly. 'She always made me feel at home when I went round.'

Not like my parents, Naomi heard the implication. She asked. 'What did your mother have against Rob? Something specific, or just the fact that he was your boyfriend?'

She felt the renewed tightening of their small but serried ranks, then Becky sighed and the trio relaxed. 'She found out I was on the pill,' she said wearily.

'Sounds sensible enough,' Naomi commented. But then, she considered, she wasn't a parent. Would that have made a difference to her attitude? Actually, she didn't think so.

Becky laughed harshly 'Listen to Mum and *Him* you wouldn't think so,' she said.

Alec arrived about an hour after Patrick and his friends had left. Naomi told him about their visit.

'You know something, don't you?' She'd been aware of the tension when she mentioned Rob Beresford's name.

Alec didn't reply straight away, he leaned forward to fondle Napoleon's ears, the big black dog wriggling with pleasure at his ministrations. 'Do you think they told you everything?'

'I doubt it. Patrick knows me, but the others don't. They're scared, Alec, they know something serious must have happened and they're thinking all sorts of stuff. I don't imagine the truth can be anything like as bad as anything they've already imagined.'

Alec said nothing.

'Can it?' Naomi demanded.

He sighed, reached out for her hand and pulled her down on to the blue sofa. 'Rob Beresford came home last night, covered in blood,' he said.

'Rob's hurt? Becky was sure the ambulance only took the mother away.'

'It did,' Alec told her. 'Clara Beresford was taken to hospital suffering from shock. We've managed to talk to her this morning. Rob arrived home just before midnight. As I say, he was covered in blood, but it wasn't his. She hugged him and it got on her clothes. It was also on the floor, on the

13

kitchen chair . . .' he paused. And added unnecessarily, 'There was a lot of blood, Naomi.'

'Do we know whose?' We. She still included herself in the equation even after nearly four years being off the force since an accident took her sight. She didn't correct herself though, knowing Alec would understand.

'Rob . . . claimed he had killed a man.'

'What?'

'According to Clara he was distressed and scared. She got him into the kitchen and he insisted she called the police. He kept telling her that he'd killed someone and . . . a body was found at three o'clock this morning. According to preliminary reports, the blood is a match. We're waiting on DNA confirmation, of course, but there seems little doubt.'

'So you've arrested Rob?' How the hell was she going to tell Patrick?

'No, no, we don't know where he is either. His mother went into the hall to call us and he ran out the back. She tried to follow but he was gone by the time she reached the gate. The paramedics found her there in a state of collapse. At first, seeing the blood on her clothes, they thought she'd been attacked, but she's not hurt, just . . .'

'Horrified,' Naomi finished. 'She must be horrified. Did Rob have any sort of record?'

'Nothing and he's doing fine at school, straight A student, expected to take the Oxbridge entrance exam. His head teacher is almost as shocked as his mother, I think.'

'God, Patrick will be . . . Do you know who the dead man is? What's the motive, do you know that yet?'

'The man is called Adam Hensel, he lives in Pinsent, so we don't know what he was doing here.' Pinsent was a half dozen miles up the coast. 'He was stabbed, single wound, but the knife had been twisted, as though the assailant tried to get it out. He bled out fast. The assailant, and for the moment Rob is our most likely suspect, must have got in close because there were no obvious defence wounds. Of course, we're waiting on the post mortem for confirmation of that. The knife was found close by; it was just a folding pocket knife, three-inch blade, nothing spectacular, but it did the job.'

14

'Was it Rob's?'

Alec shook his head. Naomi, leaning close, felt the slight movement. 'Clara Beresford says he owned a pen knife, but we found it in his bedroom. It's possible the weapon belonged to the victim, there were initials engraved on a little brass plaque on the handle. E.H. It should make it easier to identify.'

'E, not A?'

'No, but the knife wasn't new, it could have been owned by another Hensel. We don't know yet.'

'So, at least he didn't go equipped.' That was of fractional comfort. 'Can I tell Patrick any of this?'

'Not yet, no. We need to find Rob.'

'They claim he left the party around ten and they haven't seen him since. I see no reason not to believe that.'

'No, knowing Patrick, neither do I, though, obviously, I don't know his friends. What was your impression?'

'That they told me the truth about last night. That's not to say they told me everything. They were dancing around the fact that Rob hadn't been himself for the past few weeks.'

'And? They give any reason?'

'Nothing very specific. They seemed to think that Rob had been looking for his father. Apparently, Clara Beresford is a single parent and Dad was not in evidence at all.'

'But nothing more specific?'

'Um, something about him finding a letter that might have given him a clue, but no, nothing beyond that. Alec, I'd hate them to feel I was breaking confidences. Apart from anything else, it might stop them from coming back to me and I've the feeling they're not going to get much sympathy anywhere else.'

'Harry will understand,' Alec said, of Patrick's father.

'Harry will do his best, but after that incident in the summer, Harry's been having a hard time letting Patrick out of his sight. Something like this will just confirm all his fears.'

'I can understand how he feels,' Alec told her. That 'incident' Naomi referred to had seen them caught up in an armed robbery that had gone wrong. Naomi, Harry and Patrick had found themselves numbered among the hostages in a bank siege. Naomi still had bad dreams in which it was her and not her captor that had taken that final plunge from the roof.

Harry had been badly affected, feeling, quite rightly, that he had come close to losing his son. Patrick himself had gained a measure of street-cred among his peers, but it had left him scarred. He'd grown up, suddenly and too fast, withdrawn from them all. Naomi had suggested counselling and Harry had reluctantly agreed. Patrick duly spent an hour *not* talking about it every week while Harry paid for the privilege.

Now this.

'I've asked Clara to make a list of Rob's friends,' Alec said. 'They will be getting a visit, but,' he promised, 'I'll make sure the information about Rob's father came from somewhere else.'

Two

'Take your time, Mrs Beresford. I know how difficult this is.'

'Do you? Do you really?'

Alec forced himself to meet the intense gaze fixed on his own face. Clara Beresford was examining him as though looking for a particular truth; some kind of explanation. Alec couldn't help her; reasons were something he didn't have.

She pulled away, straightened her shoulders to match an already rigid back. 'I'm ready,' she told him.

How, Alec thought, could anyone ever be ready to identify the body of their son?

She studied the boy's face for so long that Alec was confused. He had attended so many of these pathetic dramas and usually, they followed a pattern. The relative steeled themselves as Clara had done, then looked at the face of the lost one for the briefest time possible, as though speed made reality less real. Occasionally, they wanted to touch, to be sure, not believing the evidence of their own eyes. Only rarely did they stare with the intensity of Clara Beresford, examine in such detail the lines and contours of the face. She reached out, not touching, but her fingers hovering uncertainly above Rob's lips.

Did she think he might still be breathing? Alec didn't know. Gently, he touched her arm. She flinched, jumped, as though he'd shocked her, her entire body registering his touch.

'What?'

'It's all right, Clara, I'm sorry; I didn't mean to startle you.'

17

'All right? How can anything ever be all right?'

Alec didn't know. 'Would you like a cup of tea? There must be things you want to ask me.'

She nodded, but didn't move. 'That's what I thought that night. Make tea, find biscuits, talk about it.' She laughed. 'Pathetic,' she almost spat the word. 'So bloody pathetic.'

She was not, he thought, a woman given to swearing. The mild expletive sounded odd coming from her lips. Who, he wondered, or what, was pathetic? Her wanting to make tea? Alec's offering it now? Or the body of her son lying in the viewing room.

'Clara.' He opened the door and this time she moved, following obediently as he left the room and took her back down the corridor to the reception area where he knew they would have the promised refreshment.

He sat her down on one of the padded chairs, pulled up a plastic one so he could sit opposite. He resisted asking her, again, if she was all right.

'Where exactly did you find him?'

'There's a bridge that crosses the road at Temple Street, just before you reach the canal basin. We think he must have gone into the water from the bridge. He was caught up in weeds just a few yards further down.'

'Gone in,' she echoed. 'Did he jump?'

'We don't know.'

'Did someone push him? How could he have fallen? I know that bridge, it has a railing. How could he have fallen?'

Hazel eyes, Alec thought. She had hazel eyes, light brown flecked with an intense green. They bored into him, searching once more for those answers he was unable to give.

'I just want to go home. Can I go home?'

Alec nodded. SOCO had finished, the officer on watch been returned to regular duty. No one had denied the neighbour's assumption that their presence had been due to a burglary. He didn't know what Clara would tell them.

'Your sister . . .'

'The blood. There was so much blood.'

'I know, Clara. I asked your sister to come here, just in case you needed someone. I hope I did the right thing?'

She nodded vaguely.

'We thought . . . we thought it might be better if you go home with her for a few days. She's packed a bag for you.'

He saw first resentment and then relief flicker across her face, the eyes harden and then blank, then grow soft as though she thought of something else, something Alec could not share.

'What happened that night,' she asked finally. 'Did he kill that man?'

Alec hesitated. 'It's too early to be sure, Clara. You're certain Rob never mentioned Adam Hensel. There's nothing you can recall. Nothing at all?'

She shook her head. 'I'd remember that name,' she said. 'It's not a usual name. Rob . . . Rob said nothing to me about an Adam Hensel.' She took a deep breath. 'When can I have the body?'

'There'll have to be a post mortem. That has been explained to you?'

She nodded. 'Yes. Will that take long?' She bit her lip hard to stop herself from crying. 'I can't bear to think of him being here, you know?'

'I know. Clara, as soon as I discover anything, I'll tell you.'

'Find out what happened,' she demanded with sudden energy. 'Why would my son kill anyone? Why would he kill someone he didn't even know? Rob was a good kid, an ordinary kid. My son isn't a killer. He isn't . . .' She could no longer hold back the tears. They poured out of her, convulsing her. Childlike, she pulled her legs up on to the chair, wrapped herself into a little ball of pain, venting a grief and torment that could no longer find its release in words.

Three

It wasn't the first time Ingham Comprehensive had played host to DI Alec Friedman and his team, but this was different. Last time Alec had conducted mass interviews it had been to collect witness statements in regard to a wanted criminal who'd been seen close to the school. This time, the focus was a dead teenager and a murdered man.

Alec had been given use of the hall and the sixth form students assembled expectantly. He'd had the chairs arranged in a rough horseshoe and seated himself in a low upholstered chair at the open end. There were one hundred and eighty-two students in the two sixth form years, apparently – years eleven and twelve as they were now officially known.

One hundred and eighty-one, now, Alec thought. Rob wouldn't be coming back.

He saw Patrick sitting two rows back between a ginger haired boy and a girl with long dark curls. Patrick was stony faced, trying not to meet Alec's gaze, perhaps not wanting to be singled out. Alec didn't think so. Patrick was open about his friendship with Naomi and Alec and it wouldn't bother him that anyone might be suspicious of his association with a police officer. No, Alec thought. Patrick was trying not to break down. The ginger haired boy next to him was staring fixedly at the corner where the ceiling met the wall in an elaborate moulding. The girl – he'd already been told her name was Rebecca Price and that she was Rob's girl-friend – was chewing on her lower lip, cheeks flushed with the effort not to cry.

Alec glanced across at the head teacher, Eileen Mathers. She nodded that everyone was here and Alec began, speaking quietly, calmly. He had already agreed with the head teacher that it would be better to give as much correct information now than have the rumours build and circulate. He had no plan to mention Adam Hensel.

'Most of you knew Rob Beresford,' he said. 'Or, at least, you knew who he was.'

Silence, a slight shifting of chairs, but nothing more.

'Rob was found dead in the canal yesterday morning at eight fifteen.' He heard someone gasp in shock, but he had also agreed there was no easy way to wrap this up. Better to say it and then let the staff and counsellors deal with the aftermath.

'We don't yet know for sure if Rob drowned, or if he died in some other way. What seems fairly certain is that he went into the water from the Temple Street Bridge, just below the canal basin. Most of you will know it; there are boats moored there now, below the weir where the factory buildings are being demolished?'

He paused again. This time a quiet murmur of agreement and recognition broke the silence.

'We know that a number of you were at a birthday party that Rob attended on the Friday night. I have a guest list from Charlie's parents and I've added a few names that Charlie tells me he invited at the last minute, but we all know what parties are like. People turn up at the last minute, tag along with friends. No one will be in trouble for that and, frankly, it's none of my concern just now, if some of you were drinking under age. This was a private function, and, to be frank, I've far more important concerns. What I do need to know is, if any of you saw Rob that night. If you spoke to him, or if any of you heard him say anything, saw him do anything, either on the Friday night or in the past few days and weeks that struck you as unusual.'

He watched again, aware that glances were exchanged, feet were shuffled; Becky Price began to cry. 'There are members of staff on hand to talk to, counsellors, should you want to talk about any of this and Mrs Mathers has agreed that should you want your parents or another adult present while you chat to myself or one of my officers, then we'll arrange that. But we do need you to talk; Rob is dead, his

21

mother had to identify the body yesterday. She needs to know how and why her son died and . . .' He hesitated. 'As things stand, there are three possibilities we have to bear in mind. One is that Rob fell, maybe he'd been drinking, maybe taking drugs. The other possibility is that someone pushed him, either by accident or maybe as a joke that went wrong; maybe even deliberately. The third possibility is that Rob . . .' He hesitated, wondering why suicide was the hardest option to talk about. 'That Rob jumped from the bridge. That he intended to kill himself and, that tragically, he succeeded in doing just that.'

Rebecca Price was sobbing now. Patrick, Alec noted, had put an arm around her shoulder and even Charlie, the ginger haired lad sitting on the other side, had torn his gaze from the ceiling and, flush faced, torn between embarrassment and concern, was leaning towards her and speaking too softly for Alec to hear.

Abruptly, Patrick got up and ushered Becky past those seated between her and freedom. Charlie dodged a swift glance at Alec and the head and then got up and followed. Alec watched as they left the hall, a teacher and a female officer following on behind.

'You must all be distressed by this,' he said gently. 'And you must have questions. I'm here. Ask me.'

He glanced again to the door; he could see Patrick and his friends through the glass panel that gave a view on to the corridor. The teacher now had her arm around the sobbing girl and the two boys stood aside, awkward and redundant. Alec turned his attention back to the assembled group. Someone, a girl three rows back, had raised a hand. The rest stared at her expectantly.

'Go ahead,' Alec told her. Other hands were inching upward into the breach she had opened. He settled back, preparing himself for the long haul.

22

Four

Alec had stopped off at the newsagent on the corner of Naomi's street. The local papers were full of Adam Hensel.

Saturday had brought a scant paragraph, stating baldly that a man had been found dead and that the police were investigating, but Monday had provided a name and exact location and that a murder investigation was now well underway.

Alec, though he had visited the scene in the early hours of the Saturday and been involved with the preliminary assessment, had since been busy with the death of Rob Beresford. Inspector Andrews was taking care of the Hensel inquiry and had made a statement on the press release: the usual stuff about investigations being ongoing and a number of leads. He had also allowed that the murder weapon had been found and that Hensel had died from a single stab wound to the chest. Death had been swift; he had bled out. Alec doubted whether even an immediate attention from medics would have made a scrap of difference.

He wondered, as he turned the key in Naomi's door, who would take precedence, himself or Andrews, when the investigations were linked as they must surely be. Frankly, he'd as soon have handed this one over; the closeness of Rob Beresford to Patrick was something he'd rather not have to deal with.

Naomi, accompanied by an enthusiastic Napoleon, greeted him at the door. She snaked her arms around his neck, pulling his head down so she could kiss his mouth. 'Mmm, better already.'

'What is?'

'My day.'

23

'Well, that's good then.' He kissed her again; she reached out curious fingers to see what he was holding under his arm.

'Newspapers? Anything about . . .? Adam Hensel's been on the national news.'

'Inevitable, I guess. I talked to the kids at the school.'

'And?'

'Not much to add to what we already knew. Rob was troubled about something and it seems likely it was to do with his father. I spoke briefly to Clara but she's refusing to say who that might have been.'

'Hmm. Helpful. She's going to have to sooner or later. It's potentially material evidence.'

'And as yet we can't be sure of that. It's all mere speculation. She didn't recognize Hensel's name, anyway.'

'You believe her?' They had made their way through to the kitchen and Naomi was measuring ground coffee into the filter.

'Do you have any biscuits? What's cooking? It smells good.'

'Biscuits are in the red tin, which . . . um, I left by the sofa come to think of it. I've made lasagne; it'll be another few minutes. You want to take care of the salad?'

'Will do.' He stomped back into the living room to find the biscuit tin. Two mugs on the coffee table, he noted. 'You had visitors?'

'A visitor, yes. Mari called in.'

'Oh?' Mari was Patrick's grandmother.

'Harry was worried about Patrick. Patrick is busy not telling his dad anything. Mari thought I might be able to fill in the gaps.'

'And?'

'I told her what she'd be able to find out in the evening papers. She's still convinced I know as much as I did as when I was on the force.'

'Well,' Alec observed. 'Most of the time, you do.'

She laughed. 'Maybe, but this time, it's a bit more . . . well, sensitive, isn't it. I want Patrick to be able to come and talk to me. He doesn't seem able to communicate with his dad at the moment.'

24

'Harry's suffering,' Alec said sympathetically.

'Oh, I know.' Naomi frowned, recalling the bank siege they had all been caught up in that summer and the fact that Patrick, who'd managed, much against his father's wishes, to escape, had come close to being shot. Harry was still having nightmares in which he lost his son. For that matter, so was Naomi. 'It's just they seem to have drifted apart these past few months. They spend so much time trying not to worry one another, they end up worrying each other because they're saying so little about anything.'

'Well, thank you Doctor Ruth,' Alec said. 'I take it you told Mari that?'

'God, Mari doesn't need telling the obvious. She's been trying to get that through to the pair of them for ages. She's actually pretty upset about it all. Patrick and Harry used to be so close.'

'They'll get over it,' Alec reassured. 'Though,' he added with feeling. 'I don't imagine any of this will help. Harry's going to be even more protective after Rob's death, especially when it comes out . . .'

'That he most likely killed Adam Hensel.' Naomi finished.

They fell silent, the kitchen quiet but for the huffing and groaning of the water through the filter. Why, Naomi wondered, did the process of making fresh coffee have to be such a noisy one, after all, it wasn't so much different from making tea. 'What do the papers say?'

'Nothing you don't know: the murder weapon's been found and that inquiries are ongoing.'

'Was he married?'

'Divorced, no kids.'

'And anything more about Rob?'

'Well, his name has been released and where he died, that drowning is suspected and police are investigating. It's all being kept very low key at the moment.'

'Hmm.' Naomi switched off the filter and reached to get mugs from the cupboard. 'That won't last. There'll be reporters crawling all over the school and his mother. All looking for an angle.'

'And Patrick, already being a little bit famous, will be an

obvious one,' Alec finished what she was thinking. 'Just what he needs.' They had managed to keep some control of Patrick's exposure during the summer by giving exclusive coverage of the siege to a journalist friend. That over, Alec and Naomi had taken an extended holiday abroad and Patrick had gone with his father to the Lakes, then on an unscheduled, but welcome couple of weeks to visit his mother and her new family in Florida. By the time they had all returned, most of it had blown over; the local press moved on to the next big thing.

Patrick had, Alec thought wryly, managed to turn his notoriety to advantage once the term started though. The rather shy and uncertain teenager found he had suddenly acquired previously unthought-of street-cred among his peers and that, coupled with the fact he'd scraped through his exams better than expected, had made – if you discounted the bad dreams – for a more comfortable term.

Until now.

'What do you think of Clara Beresford?' Naomi asked as she poured the coffee and added sugar to his. He watched, always amazed by just how competent she had become. He was sure he'd have poured scalding liquid over his hands and missed completely with the sugar. 'I like her,' he said. 'She's a tough lady. Loved her son, seems to have been open with his friends and to have had a good relationship with him.'

'But he couldn't talk to her about his father.'

'Um, no. That seems to have been the one blind spot.'

'Bit of a big one.'

'It surely was. I mean, it's natural he'd have wanted to know. She said she had no idea what letter Rob might have found.'

'You believe her?'

'No. I think she knows exactly what it was. I did wonder, though, if Rob had got hold of the wrong end of the stick and it had nothing to do with his father?'

'Oh? Reasons?'

'Feeling, nothing more. I threatened to get a search warrant if she didn't let me examine Rob's room.'

'A bit cruel?'

'I have a dead boy who'd never so far put a foot wrong but seems to have killed a man not apparently known to him. And, she was so busy not talking about Rob's father she needed something to jerk her back to the present. Oh, I know, that's the last place she wants to be, but there's also a part of her wants to know the truth no matter how much it hurts. I'm going over to the house in the morning.'

'Is it safe to leave it that long? She's not being terribly rational and, I mean that's understandable, but she might take it into her head to lose the letter.'

'I still have her keys; we used them to secure the place. And her sister, Liz, is going to call me should Clara get any ideas about going home before then. But anyway, by the time I left, I think she'd come round to the idea that she couldn't afford to hide things from me or from herself, not if she wanted to know how and why Adam Hensel and her son died.'

Five

A lec could see the relief on Clara's face that the blood had gone. Alec had seen to it that order, as much as possible, had been restored. She dropped her bag on the hall floor and walked slowly through to the kitchen.

'He sat there,' she said softly. 'In that chair. I tried . . .' Abruptly, she wheeled around and marched back into the hall. 'I'll show you his room,' she said. 'And there are some boxes in my room and stuff down here to look at. I've never known Rob go through my things, but you never know what your kids will do, do you?'

She sounded so hurt and angry that Alec felt compelled to interject, 'Clara, he was bound to be curious. It was natural.'

She nodded. A swift jerk of the head. 'I know, I know. He asked and I shut the door on him. What else could he do?'

'Why were you so adamant he shouldn't know his father? And surely, you could have claimed maintenance for him. It must have been a hell of a struggle, bringing Rob up alone.'

'We managed,' she said. 'His room's upstairs.'

She had, Alec noted, avoided his main question. He signed to the three officers with him they should wait downstairs and then followed her up the stairs. The wooden banister had been painted in white gloss, a job carried out with more enthusiasm than skill. He noted the small runs, lumpy beneath his fingers. The wallpaper had been chosen in a random pattern that needed no matching. The stair carpet was worn on the edges of the treads. He knew that these were housing association properties and that Clara had been renting here

28

for the past ten years. The house was small, clean, furnished and decorated in neutral tones. Uncluttered.

Rob's room, on the other hand . . .

'Not very tidy, I'm afraid,' Clara told him. 'But you know what teenagers are and I told him, it was his room, I wasn't going to clean it for him. He was old enough.'

She crumpled suddenly, sat down with a thump on the single bed.

'Maybe you should go downstairs?'

'No,' she shook herself, fiercely. 'I want to be here.' She took a deep breath, held it, then exhaled slowly. 'Check the desk first,' she pointed at the flat pack fake wood desk, barely visible beneath computer and magazines. 'What should I tell the others to do?'

Alec smiled at her assumption that she would be giving the orders, but he refrained from correcting her. If Clara could maintain a little of her dignity and control that way, he felt it was a small concession. 'Do you keep files? Financial, that sort of thing. School reports . . .'

She was nodding and on her feet, heading back down the stairs. Alec followed her on to the landing. In the hall below he could see her talking to the other officers, telling them that most of what they wanted to see was in the sideboard and there were some papers in her bedroom and asking if anyone would like to have tea or coffee. Sergeant Enright glanced up at Alec, raised a questioning brow. Alec just nodded. 'Sally,' he called to the policewoman, 'maybe you could help Clara sort the stuff in the bedroom and, Clara, send one of *them* into the kitchen. I could do with a cuppa.'

She nodded, smiled that tense, false smile which was the best she could manage at the moment, took another deep breath. 'Sideboard,' she said. 'The drawers, mostly. I don't know how organized . . .'

Enright, voice soft and coaxing, led her through to show him. Alec retreated to Rob's bedroom.

The room was decorated predominantly in blue and white and had about it the look of décor outgrown. There were glow stars on the ceiling and patches where others had once been. Naomi had brought some for her little nephew. He

29

didn't like the dark and the little plastic stars gave off a comforting glow for a while until he went to sleep. The curtains matched the duvet cover. Blue again, with a white strip. Grey cord carpet; what could be seen beneath the strewn clothes and yet more magazines.

Alec bent to study them. Computer games, motorbikes, music. He flicked through, checking for anything concealed between the pages, stacked them neatly in the corner, tidying as he went and adding to the heap those he'd noticed on the desk.

CDs in a wooden rack stood beside a chest of drawers. There was no wardrobe in the room, but then, Alec thought, most of his clothes seemed to live on the floor, so that probably made such a thing redundant. He opened the cases one by one, checking for anything hidden, came up empty. The bed next, turning the mattress, checking beneath, inside pillows and duvet cover. There were storage boxes beneath the bed and Alec pulled them out and checked behind them.

Straightening, Alec surveyed the room again, trying to get a feel for the boy who had inhabited this untidy, restricted space.

Clothes next. Two pairs of jeans, three T-shirts, a hooded sweatshirt and a pair of socks. Alec riffled through the pockets and lay the clothes on the already checked out bed. A survey of the drawers revealed more clothes, a couple of magazines his mother probably wouldn't want to know about, but not much else.

The boxes from beneath the bed were a little more promising being full of old schoolbooks and other assorted scraps and bits of paper. Alec took them out on to the landing ready to be taken away. They'd take time and, preferably, a couple of pairs of eyes. To his surprise, the computer didn't seem to be password protected and Alec accessed the files, skimming through essays and notes.

'I've brought you some tea,' Clara stood in the doorway.

'Thanks. Clara, do you have an internet connection?'

'Only dial up. I was always on at him not to stay on too long.' Her gaze strayed about the room, noting the stack of magazines, the clothes laid out on the bed. 'The boxes?'

30

'Full of school work, I think, but we need to go through carefully.'

She nodded. 'So you'll be taking them away.'

He nodded. 'The computer too. He might have recorded something. Did he have an email account?'

She nodded, taking a step into the room and holding out the bright blue mug of strong tea. 'He had two. One was a college one. They give all the kids the option of submitting essays online. They can use the internet or they've got an . . . intranet, is that right? In the college, between departments and tutors and such.'

The college could probably give him access to that one, Alec thought.

'Then he had his own email. I've got the address written down somewhere but I never used it.'

'Could you find it for me?'

'Yes, but you'll still need the password.'

'I'm hoping that one of his friends might know it,' Alec told her. 'Or they might be able to make a guess. Clara, why didn't you want him to know his father?'

The slight flush that touched her cheek gave him his answer. 'Clara, I don't mean to make you uncomfortable but, is it possible there was more than one candidate?'

She scowled angrily, but couldn't keep it up. Nodding sadly she told him, 'I had a boyfriend but I started seeing someone else before . . . before we split properly. It was a mistake, a stupid mistake. And I was almost certain . . . almost certain it wasn't my boyfriend that got me pregnant. He . . . We . . . we were always so careful and, when he knew I'd been two-timing him, there was one hell of a row and . . .' She gestured helplessly. 'It was all such a bloody mess. I was seventeen. Rob's age. Seems it runs in the family, doesn't it? Making a bloody mess of things?'

Rob's mess was somewhat bigger and more complicated, Alec thought. Then he wondered if it was. Did starting a new life bring with it as much fall-out in its own way as ending one? Then it seemed somehow stupid to be making such a comparison, especially as that once new life had been ended so prematurely too.

31

'So, you managed on your own,' Alec said.

'So I managed on my own. My sister was the only one wanted to know me after that. I got a place in a hostel for single mothers, fended off the social workers that wanted me to adopt, and carried on at school. I got my exams and got a job, found a child minder close by, lived in a horrid little flat, then a slightly better one and finally ended up here ten years ago. This was nice, this was home. This was where Rob did most of his growing up. This is . . .' She raised a clenched fist to her mouth, pressed it hard against her lips as though that would prevent the tears, closed her eyes.

Alec waited. Finally as she seemed to have recovered some measure of control he pursued his initial question again. 'You had no contact with either of them? Did either of the men know they might have fathered a child?'

She shrugged. 'I suppose they both knew, but I never *told* either of them they were the father. I took a mental step back and looked at them both and to be honest I suddenly could not understand what I'd seen in either. They weren't men, they were boys, not much older than me but much *much* younger in the way they acted. Though I suppose I was as bad. It was only . . . only when I had to face up to the real stuff, having a baby, being on my own, having no one to back me up and this little thing screaming for attention twenty-four hours a day. I thought about them and I thought, do I want either one of them around? And the answer was hell no. Neither was worth a damn.'

'Their families,' Alec asked. 'Did neither of the families try to get in touch? Rob must have had grandparents . . .'

Fiercely, she shook her head. 'Once,' she said. 'Once, my boyfriend's mother phoned me and she called me a slag. Mum defended me, but I knew she felt the same way. She told the woman it probably wasn't her son's anyway so what was she so bothered about and then she swore at her.' She laughed at the memory, laughter that choked and hurt in the throat. 'I never ever heard my mum swear before or since for that matter. It sounded so strange . . .'

'And you never told Rob either of their names? Did Rob know? Did Rob know there were two possibilities?'

Clara sat down again on Rob's bed. She fingered the shirt Alec had laid there, fingers running along the button band, then, absently, fastening the small blue buttons. 'He asked me,' she said. 'I told him his dad had gone away and I didn't know where.'

'And did you give him a name?'

'I gave him a name. I told him his dad's name was Andrew.'

'And was it? Clara, you have to tell me who they might have been.'

She shook her head. 'I don't *have* to tell you anything,' she said. 'The man who died, he was a stranger to us. To Rob, to me. He had nothing to do with anything in our past.'

'You don't know that, Clara.'

'And you don't know any different,' she told him pointedly. 'Look, Inspector Friedman. I know you have a job to do and I appreciate that you're trying to be as gentle with me as you can, but I didn't tell Rob about his father, far as I know I told him the truth and he *has* gone away. He certainly talked about it. Why dredge up the past now?'

'Because,' Alec said patiently, 'we have to follow every lead and Rob's friends . . .'

'Rob's friends. You place a lot of store by Rob's friends. Does their word count for more than mine? I'm telling you, this has nothing to do with Rob's father.'

Alec pulled the folding chair from beneath Rob's desk and brought it close to the bed. He sat down opposite Clara. 'I know it hurts,' he said, 'and, before you say anything more, I can't begin to comprehend how much. Frankly, I hope I'm never in the position to know how much. I don't know how I'd cope. How I'd want to go on.'

He held her gaze, that analytical, challenging look from the flecked hazel eyes. She looked for deceit, for a sign that, despite his words, he somehow diminished the full extent of her pain. 'Clara, I need to have their names. If Rob's friends are right and he went looking for his father, who knows what he might have found, or thought he found and, if he started with false information . . .'

She swallowed convulsively and then, the briefest of nods. 'I don't know where either of them is,' she said softly. 'And

that's the truth. Aiden, Aiden Ryan was the boy . . . man . . .
I two-timed with. My boyfriend was in my class at school.
His name was Jamie. Jamie Scott. There now you know and
I'd be grateful if you'd all drink your tea, take whatever you
have to take and get the hell out of here.'

Six

Charlie and Becky were already standing on the corner near the bus stop when Patrick got there.

'What do you think she wants?' he hadn't meant to sound so nervous.

Charlie shrugged.

'*They* were out, thank God,' she said, meaning her parents. 'I didn't expect her to phone me like that. It was . . . Do we have to do this?'

Patrick refrained from stating the obvious; that, evidently Becky herself thought they did seeing as she was here.

Charlie shrugged again, then turned and started to walk towards Rob's house. 'Better hear her out,' he said uncomfortably.

'What can we tell her?'

'I don't know,' Patrick said. 'What *do* we know?'

Clara must have been watching for them because she opened the door as they set foot on the front path. She stood aside to let them through and the four of them crowded into the hall, reluctant to go through the open kitchen door.

'Go into the living room,' Clara told them. 'I've got the kettle on and some biscuits and . . .' She paused and took a deep, steadying breath. 'Thank you,' she said. 'Thank you for coming. I really don't know what I was thinking of, phoning Becky like that, I must have sounded like some kind of mad woman . . .'

From what Becky had told them, Patrick thought, that was exactly what she had sounded like, but he joined the reassuring, if half-hearted murmurs of the others in their

35

attempt to reassure, though, Patrick knew, the others felt no better equipped to do this than did he.

'Clara, you go and sit down,' Becky said. 'I'll make some coffee, I know where everything is.'

Clara nodded; she seemed at the end of her strength. Charlie shot Becky a horrified look. You're leaving us to look after her? it said. Becky scowled at him and nudged Clara forward into the living room. It was Patrick that took her arm, all the time wishing he too could escape into the kitchen and telling himself that this was a bad idea. Not just bad, stupid, out of their depth idea. Glancing at Charlie he could see the same emotions writ large in the pale, pinched face and the darting eyes. Charlie wanted to turn and run and it was only loyalty to his dead friend that had brought him to see Rob's mother and that pinned him now, like an insect on a display board.

They sat in silence until Becky appeared with the laden tray.

It was strange, Patrick thought, how having something to do with your hands kind of allowed the brain to slow down and the thoughts to get in some kind of order. Surprisingly, it was Charlie that broke the silence.

'I don't know what to tell you,' he said, though so far Clara had asked nothing. 'I can't believe he threw himself off that bridge. I mean, why would he? I mean, he was all right when he left the party. He'd had a bit of a spat with Becky – sorry, Becks, but everyone could see that – I mean, he just stormed off but we all figured he'd be back to himself the next day and he'd probably not even mention it unless Becks made him and . . .'

'They think he might have killed a man.' Clara said.

Patrick stared.

'You what?' Charlie was gazing at the woman as though she really had gone mad. He stood up suddenly as though about to make a run for it, mug of coffee slipping from his hand and crashing to the floor.

Becky, mouth open, face drained of colour, placed her own mug down on the coffee table. 'Clara?'

'What the hell are you on about?' Charlie demanded.

For Patrick, more familiar with police procedure, every-

36

thing suddenly made sense: the scale of the investigation; far greater than required for a simple suicide. Horrifying as it was, it seemed suddenly obvious. 'Um, did they say who?' he blurted.

'Are you mad!' Charlie was outraged anyone could even consider the idea. 'Rob wouldn't kill anyone. I mean, fuck it, he'd go off on one occasionally, blow up and . . . and say stuff, then storm off. But he'd never . . .'

Clara replied to Patrick as though Charlie had not spoken. 'A man called Adam Hensel,' she said quietly. 'He was stabbed. When Rob came home, he was covered in blood. Adam Hensel's blood. Rob told me he had killed a man.'

'And you believe them?' Charlie still couldn't get to grips with it. 'They'll say anything. Blame anyone just so they look good. Rob wouldn't . . . Rob couldn't . . .' He sat down suddenly and for the first time seemed to be aware of the mug he had dropped. 'I'm sorry,' he said, looking at the smashed crockery and wet carpet at his feet. 'I dropped it . . . I . . .'

Charlie never cried, Patrick thought, watching as his friend finally broke down and allowed the tears to come. Charlie doesn't cry and neither do I.

It was another hour before they got around to clearing up the broken mug and spilt coffee. 'I think it's going to stain,' Becky fretted.

Clara smiled wanly. 'I'll stick a rug over it,' she said. 'That carpet's been down since we moved in anyway, it's probably time I got another one and that's nothing to the stuff Rob's . . .' She waved away the rest of the sentence.

Patrick and Charlie came through from the kitchen with fresh mugs and biscuits. Glancing at the clock above the fireplace, Patrick noted that it was after ten. He really should be heading for home. He sat back down and looked across at Clara.

'You've really never heard of him?'

Clara shook her head. 'I've racked my brains,' she said. 'And Rob's never mentioned anyone of that name to you?'

Charlie opened the biscuits. 'We'd remember a name like

that,' he said. He helped himself to three chocolate diges-
tives, then paused. 'Is it OK,' he said. 'I'm starving.'

Clara's smile was genuine this time. 'Maybe I could make
sandwiches?'

They exchanged glances. What was it about grief, Patrick
wondered, that made you not want to eat and then suddenly
ravenous.

'Um, no, it's all right,' Charlie began.

'Look, I'd like to. It would be kind of . . . normal.'

Patrick picked up the tray again. 'We'll all help,' he said.
'What else did the police take away?'

It felt strange, he thought, to be talking about 'police' in
the abstract, when he now knew it had been Alec that had
carried out the search.

'Those two boxes, his computer, mobile phone, that sort of
thing.' She shrugged. 'To be honest, I stopped watching after
a while. I just couldn't bear it. They were hoping one of you
would know the password to his email account, I think.'

'I know what it *was*,' Charlie mused. 'But he was always
changing it. Usually to something stupid. I don't think he
used it that much anyway, we all used to text or use *chat*
online.'

'He didn't mention anyone. Anyone else he might have
been in contact with?'

'Nothing.' Becky told her. 'I wish he had.'

Patrick was thinking hard. 'Rob wasn't secretive,' he said.
'I mean, he could never keep anything to himself, could
he. You'd tell him something and next minute he'd blurt it
out, then get all defensive when he remembered he'd been
meant to keep his mouth shut. Oh,' he added, seeing the
sudden anxiety in Clara's eyes. 'I don't mean big stuff, I
mean . . .'

'Like if someone fancied someone,' Becky explained.
'You'd never tell Rob, not unless you wanted everyone to
know. He just didn't think.'

Clara nodded, recognizing the trait. 'But you think there
was something. Something he'd been keeping back?'

Patrick nodded.

'Yeah,' Charlie agreed reluctantly. 'He seemed edgy, impatient, got into rows with Becky and that wasn't normal. Rob didn't like rows, they were too much bother.'

'But you don't know what?'

Charlie sighed. 'He talked about his dad a time or two,' he said. 'I mean, he'd talked about him before, about how he wondered who he was and sometimes . . . sometimes he got really annoyed that you wouldn't tell him anything.'

'And he said something about a letter he'd found,' Becky added suddenly.

'Found?'

Becky looked embarrassed. She looked to the others for support.

'Becky,' Clara said patiently. 'Do you honestly think anything you could tell me now would be worse than what I already know?'

Impulsively, Becky reached out and grasped Clara's hand. 'No,' she admitted. 'I don't suppose it would be. I just . . .' She laughed nervously, 'God this'll sound stupid. I don't want anyone to think badly of him, you know?'

Clara patted her hand. 'I know,' she said. 'Have you told the police anything you've not told me?'

They shifted uncomfortably. 'No,' Becky said. 'We told them Rob had said something about a letter.'

'I think that's what they came here looking for.'

'But we don't know what letter. Rob didn't say where he'd got it, but he said . . .' She took a deep breath. 'He said he'd got pissed off because you wouldn't talk to him about his dad, he said he had a right to know. We think, we think he went through your stuff one day when you were out.'

'We only think that,' Charlie added. 'We really didn't know.'

Clara nodded. She crossed to the cupboard and fridge and began to assemble the ingredients for sandwiches. They moved to help her, getting in one another's way but glad of something to do. That magic of having your hands working, Patrick thought.

'Do you know what the letter was?' he asked shyly.

Clara paused, butter knife poised above bread. 'No,' she said. 'That's the thing. I shut all of that out of our lives, burned letters, threw out old photos. As far as I know, there was nothing there for Rob to have found.'

39

Seven

It was past midnight by the time Patrick arrived home and he knew he'd be in trouble. They had an agreement that on school nights Patrick would be home by eleven and, if he was likely to be late, he should call Harry and tell him. It was an agreement that cut both ways; Harry, Patrick's dad, would never dream of leaving Patrick to worry should he be running late or have to change his plans. Patrick had switched his mobile off when they'd gone to see Clara; he'd completely forgotten to either switch it on or tell his dad when he might be back.

Patrick and his dad shared a small terraced house about forty minutes walk from Rob's place. The front door opened straight into the living room. Harry sat, television turned down, newspaper spread out on his lap, though Patrick could tell that neither the television nor the paper had held his attention in quite some time.

Do you even know what's on? Patrick wanted to ask, Instead, he offered, 'Sorry I'm late,' hoping that would do.

Harry didn't move. 'I was worried about you,' he said. 'Where did you go?'

'Out. Just out.'

'It's past twelve. You can't have been "just out" all this time.'

Patrick could both hear and feel the degree of control Harry was exercising just to keep his voice steady. Remorse and irritation – what right had his dad to make him feel guilty? He'd done nothing wrong – fought it out in Patrick's head. 'I was with Charlie,' Patrick said. 'And Becky.'

'I called Charlie's parents. They didn't know where you were either.'

'You did what?' Irritation won. 'You checking up on me?'

'You didn't call, your phone was off. I told you, I was worried.'

'I don't need you checking up on me.'

Harry got out of his chair and faced his son. 'And I don't need to be sitting here, worried sick. Anything could have happened. Anything.'

'Nothing happened,' Patrick stared sullenly at his feet. Guilt had been tagged by conscience and had now entered the ring. 'I was just out, that's all.'

Harry took a deep breath. 'Where did you go to? Am I at least allowed to know that?'

Patrick shrugged. He wondered how Becky and Charlie's parents were reacting now. Charlie, being a nominal adult, had parents who were pretty flexible about his comings and goings, but he could imagine Becky's mum and step-dad would be less than pleased to know where their daughter had been. Harry rarely lost his temper. Sometimes, Patrick almost wished he would, then he could shout back, feel justified in being angry.

'Patrick?' Harry prompted.

Patrick sighed. 'Becky got a phone call,' he said. 'Charlie and me, we went with her.'

'Went where? A phone call from . . .?'

Wearily, Patrick threw himself into his father's recently vacated chair. Harry hesitated for a moment and then settled on the sofa opposite and Patrick knew that he was partly off the hook. Harry wasn't about to yell at him or get mad or interrogate or any of the things Patrick half wished he'd do. Harry was preparing to listen and in a strange sort of way, Patrick found that even harder. It meant he had to talk, to explain, to . . .

'We went to see Rob's mum,' he said. 'She called Becky, wanted to talk to her, and to Charlie, I suppose. Becky said she wished she hadn't rung at home, knowing how Becky's mam and step-dad felt about Rob, but they were out and I guess she didn't want to go alone, so I suppose she just asked Charlie and me to go along and . . .'

He was rambling, making no sense what so ever. He wanted

41

his bed. He wanted his dad to ask him the right questions so he didn't have to go through the whole thing again like they had with Clara. He wanted to be left alone.

He lifted his gaze and stared at his dad, not sure which of those things he desired most and hoping that Harry would make the choice for him. Then all he'd have to do was respond. Though, Patrick wasn't even sure he could do that very well right now.

Harry met his gaze and held it. He, being Harry, didn't do any of the things Patrick had anticipated. Instead, he said quietly, 'When my sister disappeared, my mother . . . she wanted to talk to anyone and everyone who might have seen or talked to her or known anything. Even the most stupid little thing. She would hang around outside the school gates, waiting. I suppose for Helen, I don't know. I think she hoped . . . half believed my sister would come out of the school with the other children and the nightmare would be over.'

Patrick was distracted. 'Nan did that?'

Harry nodded. 'The other parents, they tried to understand. To be patient with her, but she did it, day after day, standing there as the children came out, demanding to know if they'd seen her child, if they knew anything. The parents complained to the head teacher and to the police. She was, they said, frightening their children, but you know, I think really, she was frightening them.'

'Them? How?'

Harry smiled sadly, recalling just how distraught and desperate his mother, Mari, had been. 'I think, you know, that she was quite unhinged for a while.'

'Nan?' Mari was one of the sanest, most sensible and ordered people Patrick could think of.

'But the other parents, they were . . . afraid, I think. It was as though they feared . . . contamination. Tragedy, especially a tragedy that involves a child, it brings home to you just how precious and fragile your loves and lives can be and, however sympathetic people are, however much they care and give their support, they are still afraid. They think, it's happened once; might it not happen again?'

'And do you feel like that?' Patrick wanted to feel aggrieved

42

if Harry did, but at the same time, he felt awed by the revelation, as though suddenly privy to some shameful secret of the adult world.

Harry nodded. 'I'm ashamed to say that a little part of me does feel that way,' he said. 'A little part of me wants to know what it was that went wrong in your friend's life that made him do what he did. To kill yourself; to take your own life . . . frankly, Patrick, I find it hard to comprehend. Helen, my little sister, her life was taken from her. She didn't have any say in the matter or any power to change things. Oh,' he added, looking at the turmoil written on his son's face, 'I'm not judging your friend. For someone so young to be in such despair is a thing that should never happen. Never, in a million years.'

He paused, left the silence as an invitation to his child, but Patrick shook his head, unable to fill it. What could he say? Rob killed himself because he'd killed another person? How could Harry be expected to react to that? Patrick just couldn't bring himself to speak the words out loud.

'I'm tired out, Dad,' he said at last. 'I need to go to bed.'

Mutely, Harry nodded. 'His mother must be . . .'

'Yeah,' Patrick told him, 'yeah, she is.' He left the room, the tightness in his throat preventing him from saying more. Harry's following gaze seemed to be drilling a hole right into his stiffened back.

Across town a girl lay wakeful in her bed. Jennifer was seventeen. She was also pregnant, though not enough yet that it showed; not unless you really looked hard.

Creased in her hand was the front page of the local paper. She had gazed at the image so long and so hard that if she closed her eyes, it seemed imprinted on the inside of the lids. And, as she stared up at the ceiling, the shadow of it danced before her eyes like a projection in the dark.

The picture was of Robert Beresford. Now deceased, believed to have fallen from a bridge into the canal and died among the weeds and dumped shopping trolleys and filthy, muddy water. The picture had been taken at the school prize

43

giving the year before and Rob, clutching a book, smiled out self-consciously.

Jenny liked his smile. She had always liked his smile.

She turned over on her side, trying to block the images that swam before her eyes, images that seemed magnified by the unshed tears.

Eight

As predicted there had been a fair amount of media interest in and around the school, though Eileen Mathers, the head teacher, had done everything in her power to keep them off school premises, threatening legal action should anyone trespass.

She had been particularly concerned for those of Rob's friends who were at the school and might be identified. The suicide of a promising student made good copy. She had issued a statement on behalf of the school. The usual phrases of 'tragic loss, a life cut short too soon, a bright, popular and happy boy'. Naomi had heard it on the lunchtime news. She had heard too in the voice of this head teacher, a woman used to dealing with the squalls and storms of adolescent angst, that she was deeply and personally shocked by this particular death and that the words, however clichéd, were sincerely meant.

Naomi was sincerely relieved that the connection between Rob's death and that of Adam Hensel had not been publicized. She had no doubt that the media would make the connection, but hoped that there would be bigger, more certain news to fill their pages and that Rob and his family and her friends would be left in peace.

It was with relief also that only one paper made the connection between Patrick and the siege and Rob, and then it was to make only some bland comment about tragedy in young lives and the stresses our modern teenagers were under. Naomi didn't quite see the connection between being held hostage and the strains of teenage years, but if that was all they had to say, she was willing to let it lie.

'How are you getting on with it?' Patrick asked. She was

still playing with the voice activated software he'd persuaded her to buy. In theory, it meant that she could use her computer unaided. So far, it had proved to be more trouble than it was worth. She had spent the required amount of time training it – she began to think it had taken less time to train Napoleon – and had duly repeated the lessons when it still failed to comply with her voice commands. Patrick had suggested it might need more RAM and gave her an extended lecture on how temporary files were created every time she did anything and information was constantly being swapped . . . or something.

'Better today. Your idea has made a difference. Look, I wrote a letter and listened through read back. It almost makes sense.'

Patrick came and peered over her shoulder. 'Cool. Most of it is actual words.'

Naomi laughed. 'Yeah, but you watch this.'

She switched on the microphone and spoke into it, 'Internet.'

The screen changed and the machine logged on.

'Browse.' She turned away from the microphone. 'See. Soon I'll be able to shop online.'

'Brilliant. You tried it yet?'

'Well, no, actually, that's as far as I got, but it's better than nothing. I have hit a problem though.'

'What?'

'I'm going to have to memorize a whole heap of web addresses.'

'Maybe you should persevere with the Braille. I expect there are directories.'

'Braille *smail*. Patrick, I'll never get that. There's got to be another way. You did better than I can.'

'Yeah, but I have less years to unlearn.' He dodged out of the way before she realized she'd been insulted. 'Guess what. No reporters outside the school today.'

'Oh, that's good. Obviously something more interesting going on. I heard there was a big fire, warehouse or something up by the docks. Maybe they've gone up there. How's things generally, anyway?'

46

'Oh, you know. It still doesn't make sense. I nearly got into a row with Dad last night.'

'What did you do?'

He hesitated, sat down on the floor near her computer table and leaned back against the wall. Napoleon huffed down on top of him. 'We went to see Clara. Rob's mum. She asked us to.'

'Did Harry object to that?'

'No. I got back late and I didn't phone. Naomi, has Alec talked to you about stuff? About Rob, I mean.'

She nodded. 'Patrick, where is this leading?'

'Clara told us something, but I didn't tell Harry, I didn't know how and he was worried enough last night and, well, it didn't seem to be the right time. But then, I got to thinking today and I don't think there'll ever be a right time, so I think I've got to tell him tonight. Naomi, I don't know how.'

'Clara told you about Adam Hensel.'

'Yeah. She did.' He waited and then he asked what he really wanted to know. 'Do you think he did? Kill this man, I mean.'

Naomi sighed. 'You want me to talk to your dad?' she asked him.

'That sure,' Patrick said. 'Why?'

'Because all of the evidence points that way. Adam's blood on Rob. Rob's prints on the knife. No evidence, at least yet, of anyone else on the scene. That's why.'

He said nothing and Naomi wondered if she should be the one to break the silence. Finally, it was Patrick who spoke out. 'Can you tell my dad,' he asked her. She could tell from his voice that he was trying not to cry.

47

Nine

The inquest into Rob's death had been opened and adjourned, though it had been agreed that his body could be released for burial and it was tacitly understood that a verdict of suicide was likely to be the eventual one. Toxicology reports revealed both narcotics and alcohol in his bloodstream. The miracle was that he'd made it to the bridge at all.

It was a factor Clara had problems in squaring with her memory of her son on that night. He'd been distressed, certainly, despairing. But drunk? No. High? She didn't think so.

Nothing had been found in the search carried out at her home and Charlie had been adamant that Rob, though he might get drunk occasionally, didn't do drugs. Patrick backed him up with similar vehemence.

It was only Becky that cast doubt. 'The past week or so,' she said 'he'd got himself involved in other stuff.' She either really didn't know or didn't want to say what. 'It was one of the things we'd rowed about the night of Charlie's party. Mum and *him* were already down on Rob. If he'd turned up at my place the way . . . the way he was when we met up the night before Charlie's party . . .'

'One of the things you argued about?' Patrick asked her but Becky must have felt she'd betrayed Rob's memory enough already. She shrugged her shoulders and looked away. Patrick knew he'd get nothing more from her.

The funeral was a quiet, empty affair. Naomi and Harry attended with Patrick. Harry, to support his son and Naomi because she felt drawn in by her association and because she knew just how much Harry hated funerals. They reminded him too much of the memorial they had for his sister, Helen, and, later, much, much later, Helen's funeral. They, apart from Clara and the odd neighbour, were the only adults present.

Why, Naomi wondered, did they so often sing 'All Things Bright and Beautiful' at funerals? They had, she recalled, sung the hymn at Helen's and at her father's. She mumbled the words, remembering them well enough from long ago school assemblies. Beside her, Harry intoned with more emotion than accuracy and Patrick was silent, his arm pressed close against hers. She could feel him shaking. Napoleon nuzzled at her hand, sensing that his people were upset and ill at ease. She felt Patrick's hand brush hers as he reached down to fondle the dog's silky ears.

A little distance away, a woman wept, her sobs a constant backdrop to the singing and then to the eulogy which spoke of lost opportunity and a life cut short too soon. As if we needed telling that, Naomi thought.

There was to be no wake.

Charlie and Becky joined them outside, and Patrick stepped away from his father and Naomi to speak to them, their voices hushed as though overcome by the solemnity of the moment.

'I should be going,' Harry said uneasily. 'I can stay,' he added, addressing his comment to his son.

'No, Dad, you'd better go. You've got that meeting and stuff. Look,' he added, 'thanks for coming. I'm glad you did.'

'I'm glad too,' Harry told him. 'You sure you'll be OK? How are the three of you getting back to . . . wherever?' It was a school day, but Harry wasn't so naïve he thought that's where they'd go.

'We'll be OK, thanks,' Charlie answered for them. 'We'll walk back home, I think. We can go back along the towpath.'

'The towpath?'

Naomi could feel Harry force back the protest. The canal was where Rob had died, where . . . other bad things had happened. 'OK, then,' he managed, his voice just fractionally unsteady. 'Nomi? You want for me to call a taxi? Or I could give you a lift?'

'I can do that,' a woman's voice. 'I'm Rob's mother,' she added. 'Clara Beresford. I just wanted to thank you. For coming along. All of you.'

Not many had, Naomi thought. The echoing emptiness of the crematorium and the few voices raised to praise the 'Bright and Beautiful' had told her that. She wondered if Clara had invited others or chosen not to. Clara's voice was thickened by the tears she had shed.

'You must be Naomi,' Clara said quietly. 'And Harry, Patrick's father.'

Harry confirmed his identity and repeated his excuses. He kissed Naomi on the cheek and checked again that she would be alright to get home.

Naomi found herself walking down the path from the crematorium, Patrick and his friends behind and Clara at her side.

'I really am so sorry,' she said. 'I can't imagine what you must be going through.'

'I don't know what's worse,' Clara told her candidly, 'losing my son or knowing he killed someone else's. It's all right,' she added, 'Patrick told me you knew. It's a relief, actually, feeling I can say something. Everyone has been so nice, so sympathetic, and I feel almost like a fraud. If they suspected . . . My God, if they knew.'

'We don't know what happened,' Naomi reminded her. 'Not yet. There could have been some kind of accident.'

'It could have been,' Clara agreed. 'But, frankly, it doesn't seem like it, does it, and everyone's going to draw their own conclusion sooner or later, aren't they? I mean, the papers have reported the police know who killed Adam Hensel and that the killer is believed to have committed suicide. You won't need to be a rocket scientist to figure it out even if they aren't allowed to print Rob's name.'

'Are you scared of reprisals?' Naomi asked her. 'The police can give you protection if you feel threatened; you know that, don't you.'

Clara laughed harshly. 'No policeman can protect me from

my own thoughts,' she said. 'No one can take the bad dreams away. You know, my family, what's left of them, *they* didn't even bother to come today. Didn't want to be involved. Not that they've ever been involved in Rob's life anyway. Too bloody ashamed of me for that.'

'Ashamed of you?'

'For having Rob. For not having married his father, regardless.'

Regardless of what, Naomi wondered. 'There are a lot of single parents,' she protested. 'It's not such a big thing in this day and age.'

'No? No, not to most people. Just to my bloody lot. I told my sister not to come,' she admitted. 'She wanted to, but I know what hell Mam would put her through if she did, she's not been right since Dad passed on. Everything got worse after that. God, listen to me, giving you my life history, aren't I?' She tried to laugh and Naomi smiled in her direction. 'I just can't seem to think straight.'

'I'm not surprised.' Naomi told her.

They paused, having reached the gates and the parked cars.

'Nomi, we're going back to Charlie's place,' Patrick told her. 'Is Clara giving you a lift home?'

'I said I would,' Clara confirmed. 'That is, if it's OK with Naomi. I don't want to seem to be organizing you.'

'No, a lift would be welcome,' Naomi told her. 'If it's not putting you out.'

'Not at all and the truth is, I've got some things to ask. Patrick thought you might be able to help me out.'

'I can try,' Naomi told her cautiously. 'But you've got to understand, I'm probably no more in the loop than you are.'

'I know. I just need to know what will happen now,' Clara said. She had helped Naomi into the front passenger seat. Napoleon sprawled happily in the back. 'I mean, the police have said they aren't looking for anyone else, but that the case is still open. Why?'

She wants it all to be over, Naomi thought. Over, closed, put away so she can start to grieve for her boy and put out of her mind the reasons he jumped off that bridge.

'I know they found that man's blood all over Rob. Rob's

51

fingerprints were on the knife that killed him. He confessed. He's dead. What further punishment . . . what more can they do? Can't they just . . . What more do they want to know?'

Naomi hesitated, caught between compassion for this woman and the need – Clara's need too – for her to give a straight reply.

'Why?' she said softly. 'We might know that Adam Hensel died and that in all probability Rob killed him, but Clara, what the police need to know now, is *why*. *You* need to know why. You'll never be able to get over this unless you do. And,' she added, gently, 'don't you think Adam Hensel's family deserve to understand that just as much as you do?'

Ten

After a crisis, Naomi thought, you get to make a choice. You either cling to the old and the familiar as if it were moulded into some kind of clumsy, misshapen life preserver, or you draw a line, step over it and leave as much of the past as you feasibly can.

She'd be the first to acknowledge that both the line and the leaving were largely symbolic. The same people – with a few additions – were important to her now as they had been before she went blind. In fact, many of those relationships had deepened. Conversely, others had been abandoned altogether.

Similarly, after the bank siege, having dealt with the genuine fear that they would not get out alive, Naomi had drawn another line, crossed it and left behind any part of herself not determined to live life to the absolute max. Unfortunately, the Naomi that had moved on was also possessed of, or possessed by, a dissatisfaction that the old Naomi would never have given house room to. She was restless, irritated, unable to settle.

Post traumatic stress, Alec called it. Mari wondered, tentatively, if she might be depressed, an irony that was not lost on Naomi. After all, she had no right, did she, to be depressed or self-indulgent; she was alive and safe and loved and it could all have been very different. Or perhaps that was the problem? Was she so conscious of the need to be grateful and for her every action to be life-affirming that she somehow felt she was cheating or cheapening the experience should she, even for a moment, forget to be either?

She recognized a similar sense of confusion in Patrick.

53

It had been present after the bank siege. It was heightened now. Patrick, though, was trying the opposite tack. While Naomi, to Alec's horror, signed up to do a tandem charity skydive and wondered if she could find a salsa class that could cope with someone not only blind but totally lacking in that kind of co-ordination, Patrick immersed himself in the ordinary and the mundane. For the first time in his school career, he was up to date with his assignments and didn't have to be nagged to get his homework done. Harry, while glad that Patrick's grades were improving, nonetheless admitted his anxiety; it didn't seem normal, at least, not for Patrick. And, while previously he'd been someone content with his own company, Patrick now hated to be alone in the house. After school, when not with his friends, Patrick inevitably showed up at Naomi's flat. The third time she came back to find him sitting on the wall outside, she went and got him a key cut. He could, he said, cope with her flat. It was small, there was nothing upstairs. He could look out and see the sea if he cricked his neck sideways and, as if it were relevant, she had a filter coffee machine.

His visits, always frequent, became so commonplace that Harry would now stop off on his way home to collect his son, knowing that their house would be empty.

This was not normal either. Not for Patrick.

'Do you still have bad dreams?'

It was rare for Harry to accept her offer of coffee. Usually he just called in to say hello, check that she was all right, gather Patrick's belongings and leave for home, eager to get a meal and a rest after a long day. Today, though, he had accepted the coffee and seated himself next to his son on the old blue sofa.

Naomi heard Patrick shift, his feet scuffing the floor as he reacted in surprise to his dad's question.

'Bad dreams. You mean about the siege?' she asked.

'The siege, and other things.'

Helen. He meant Helen, Naomi thought. She nodded slowly. 'Yeah, sometimes. I find it harder to sleep. The smallest thing wakes me.' She laughed. 'Not that Alec notices; he sleeps like the dead.' She regretted the simile even as it escaped. She heard Patrick stand up.

'We ready then?'

'Your dad hasn't finished his coffee,' Naomi said gently. Patrick sat back down.

'What makes you ask?' It wasn't a Harry sort of question.

'I don't know. I suppose, because *I* still do. I suppose I wanted to know if that was normal.'

'I think it probably is.' She paused. 'Sometimes, I wake up and I'm back there, locked in, waiting . . . just waiting. I have to put the light on, check the time, make sure I'm back in my own bed in my own room.'

'You put the light on?' Harry was intrigued.

'Old habits, I guess. It's still the first thing I do when I come home. I can, just, tell the difference, if I stare straight at it.'

'I dreamt about Rob last night,' Patrick said and Naomi understood what this was all about.

'You often dream about Rob,' Harry said gently.

Patrick sounded shocked. 'How do you know?'

'Sometimes, you call out his name.'

Naomi could feel Patrick's shock at this exposure. She wondered what she should say.

'Look, I think I'd like to go home now,' Patrick got in first. 'See you on Monday, Naomi. If that's OK?'

'Of course.' She heard him get up again and cross the room to the corner where he'd dumped his bag and coat.

Harry got up to follow his son. He bent down to kiss Naomi on the cheek.

'Go slowly,' she breathed. 'Don't push it, Harry.'

She felt him nod, then the footsteps across the room, the door close, the front door slam.

Did she still dream? Oh yes. Panicked dreams where she searched in vain for her friend Helen. Dreams in which she was a child again, lost and confused and very, very scared. Sometimes the dream child would wander into the armed siege. The child in Naomi crying with fear as the shots rang out and the men's voices were raised in threat and anger, and the worse thing was, she didn't even need to be sleeping for the dreams to come.

'You want to talk about it?' Harry asked. He reached to switch on the radio. Experience had told him that distraction, such as listening to music, could make it easier for his son to relax.

'Not really, thanks anyway.' Patrick was trying hard to sound mature and off hand.

'OK, then,' Harry told him. Experience had also told him, and Naomi reminded him, that pushing too hard was likely to have the opposite to the desired effect. 'Well, I'm here. Naomi's always ready to listen too, you know that. And there's your counsellor.'

'Her,' Patrick snorted. 'Dad, I don't know why you keep paying for her. All she does is sits me down and waits for me to "open up" to her. Like that's going to happen.'

'She seems pleased with your progress,' Harry said mildly.

'Oh, sure she is. She's pleased with the money you keep paying her, whether she does any good or not.'

'Or whether you turn up or not?'

'Whether I . . .' Patrick sighed and reached to change the channel on the radio.

To Harry's surprise, he settled on a station playing jazz. Harry listened, trying to place the piece. 'What is that?' the question was self-addressed, but his son answered.

'It's Miles Davis,' he said. '"Angel Eyes". It's on that compilation Nan bought you for your birthday.'

'Oh yes, so it is. I didn't know you liked it.' He turned to glance at his son.

Patrick shrugged. He was staring hard out of the side window. Harry could see his reflection in the shadowed glass. The face, tight and pinched. Emotion dangerously close to the surface. 'I like all sorts of stuff, you know that.'

'Well, yes. I suppose you do.'

They listened in a silence that was almost companionable, then when the last notes of 'Angel Eyes' tailed away Patrick asked, 'Do you think you could kill someone?'

Harry flinched at the question. Asked for a description of

Harry, most people would use words like 'mild mannered' or 'even tempered', but . . . 'Yes,' he said. 'I believe I could. If someone threatened those I love, I believe I could take their life, or maim or injure and not even hesitate.'

He half felt, half heard his son release the breath he had been holding and wondered at the cost of asking that question. It saddened him. He and Patrick had once been able to discuss anything, trade ideas and bad jokes, be peaceful and happy in one another's company. Oh, Harry knew how to behave when Patrick was around his college friends. Then, if you were a sensible parent, you took a back seat and kept yourself just a little bit apart. He remembered his own embarrassments at the hand of his beloved mother, Mari, when he'd been Patrick's age. He didn't think he'd done too badly in comparison.

'I know I could,' he corrected himself. 'Patrick, if I'd had a weapon during that siege . . . I know I would have used it. Believe me; I'm not comfortable with that little piece of self knowledge.'

Patrick nodded. He was, Harry noted, now staring fixedly out of the front windscreen. They turned into their road and pulled on to the drive, though, by some tacit consent, made no move to get out of the car.

'I know I could have then,' Patrick said quietly. 'And that kind of scared me, you know?' He turned to look at his father, eyes fixed and intense, searching for confirmation, understanding.

Harry nodded. 'As I said, I'm not comfortable with that either, but Patrick, I think of all those ordinary men and women who have had that decision, that . . . acknowledgement thrust upon them. In war or in danger or . . . whatever. It's kind of comforting, knowing that they must have found it just as hard. Just as revelatory and just as distasteful and uncomfortable. I can't believe many people kill easily. I can't believe many actually become immured to it. Maybe even get to enjoy it.'

'You've thought about it a lot, then.'

Harry nodded. 'I don't think there's a day gone by I haven't considered it. I've not tried to convince myself that I'm different.'

'Different?'

'From the man who murdered Helen. From the men who held us hostage.' Harry shrugged. 'Just *different from . . .*'

'Rob was *different from*,' Patrick said slowly. 'Dad, I've thought about it so much and I'm certain now. Rob would never just go and kill someone he didn't know. Not even as an accident, he, just wouldn't.'

'Accidents, by their very nature, aren't preventable or predictable,' Harry said cautiously, not really understanding where Patrick was going with this.

'No, I know that,' Patrick's voice carried an edge of impatience and Harry, wisely, made no comment that might put him off further from getting his thoughts out. 'I've thought about it a lot and I think . . . I know . . . that's what Rob must have been doing. Protecting someone else. Someone he cared about.'

Harry frowned. His first instinct was to tell Patrick he was clutching at straws; trying to make sense of the incomprehensible. He bit down on the impulse to voice this, knowing it was a sure fire way to stop Patrick in his tracks.

'Who?' he asked. 'You don't think Becky might have followed him? Been there . . .'

Patrick was shaking his head vehemently. 'No, not Becks,' he said. 'She wasn't there. No, someone else, someone . . . we don't know about and the police don't know about.'

Harry considered. 'Alec would have said if there was evidence of a third person.'

Patrick shook his head. 'No one was looking, were they?' he asked bleakly. 'They've got a dead body and someone to blame for it. Not even Alec cares about anything more than that.'

Eleven

It seemed to Jennifer that the whole world had Christmas on the brain. She hadn't attended college much in the past month; morning sickness that lasted all day and fear of the looks, the sly nudges now she was starting to show, had contrived to keep her at home. In the end, her mum had given up trying to make her go. Her form tutor had kept in touch, though and was still sending her work in the hope she'd change her mind and there had been talk, for the New Year, of placing her in a specialist unit set up for girls in her position.

'In her position', Jennifer thought. Seventeen, pregnant, disapproved of. The more so since her utter refusal to name the dad. Her own father had gone all macho on her and stormed round to the home of every boy he even suspected of looking the wrong way at her – behavior that had not exactly helped on the college front. But he had drawn a blank as she had known he would.

After that, his fury had seemed to dissipate, transmuting, instead, into a grudgingly uncomfortable silence. He seemed, now, Jennifer thought, to be going out of his way to ignore her expanding belly, while her mother, ever the practical one, had been looking round for the best deals on baby paraphernalia. The spare room, destined to become the nursery, was already stacked with packs of nappies.

Jennifer, hearing a car door slam, glanced out of the window, surprised she had not heard the engine. She saw her aunt get out of the car and her parents' 4 x 4 pull round it and on to their drive.

Jennifer sighed. She'd been spared the funeral, but the wake was going to be as bad, if not worse; relatives and friends no doubt dividing themselves into the two parental camps: ignore the fact that she was pregnant or offering unwelcome advice.

Truthfully, Jennifer was unsure which was worse.

The front door opened and her mother called up to her. Reluctantly, Jennifer left the sanctuary of her room. She paused on the landing, sitting for a moment on the top step to gaze down into the hall, remembering the many times she'd done that as a child, sent to bed while the family party still went on downstairs, sharing in the noise and laughter of the adults, though at one remove. As she'd got older and bedtimes been delayed, she had been allowed to share in the grown-up gossip and discovered that, in fact, it often got quite boring. Parents and relatives getting slowly more inebriated – though never to the point of disgrace; her mother would never have countenanced that – and talk turning to politics or sport or long-dead strangers that Jennifer had never known. She had, almost, longed to be back on the stairs, catching the snatches of conversation and Uncle Adam's shouts of raucous laughter. The little treats he'd sneak out to her, while her mother pretended not to notice.

Once, when she'd been about ten, and he more sauced than usual, he had brought her a glass of cherry brandy. Liking the taste, she'd drunk it like pop and asked him for more. She tried to recall if he'd obliged, but couldn't. She bit her lip and fought down the urge to cry.

Here, at the head of the stairs, she was almost on a level with the tinsel star set atop the tall tree. December the twenty-first, time to begin the celebrations and the tree had been set up as usual, delivered by the friend of her dad's who owned the Christmas-tree farm, and set carefully in its pot guided by her father's instructions. Even her uncle's death was not allowed to interfere with such a family tradition.

She and her mother had trimmed it last night ready for the arrival of today's guests, almost as if this were just another family celebration, the usual coming together of the generations. It was possible to forget . . . no, not quite, seeing her mother dressed in formal black and her father in the suit that came out only on such solemn occasions and Aunt Carol's

60

inappropriately bright red hair covered with a sober blue scarf. No, not really possible to forget that this was not some pre-Christmas ritual, but was instead the wake for a murdered man.

'How was the funeral?' Naomi asked.

'It was a funeral.' Alec pulled her close and planted a kiss on her nose.

'Yeuk. Now a proper one.' She wiped her face on his shirt. 'Anything useful happen?'

'Well,' he released her and bent down to fuss Napoleon. 'I don't know that there was a lot useful left to expect. The family were glad to finally be able to bury their dead and, I think, were mollified by the fact we had sent representatives, but disappointed we were no further on.'

'You still don't know why Rob killed him,' Naomi said.

'No, and frankly, I think that's the way it's going to stay. Case solved, move on.'

'But it isn't solved.'

'We're not looking for anyone else. The investigating team's been broken up and reassigned. It's about as solved as it's going to get.' He sighed, flopped down on the blue sofa and dragged Naomi beside him. 'You know the score; it's all a matter of allocating resources.'

'It isn't right,' Naomi objected.

'Right doesn't even come into it. How's Patrick? Did he turn up this evening?'

'No, actually he's gone to the pictures with Charlie and Becky, some others too, I think. Term ended at lunchtime.'

'Ah, right, I was forgetting that.'

'And what have you been doing with your day?'

Naomi stretched and wriggled into a more comfortable position, plonking her legs down across his lap. 'Foot massage, please. I met Mari and my sister, in Pinsent, no less, and we finished off the Christmas shopping.'

'Pinsent?'

'Yep and I caught the bus.'

'I'm impressed.'

'So you should be. We're talking about going to London for the sales. What do you think?'

'I think I should hide your credit cards.'

'Bit late for that.' She wriggled her toes. Strong fingers dug into the soles of her feet, applying just enough pressure to be almost painful but immensely relieving. 'Um, feels good. What are they like? Adam Hensel's family. Unusual name.'

'I think it's Dutch, or German, maybe. Adam's father was an immigrant in the 1950s, I believe. Adam and his sister were born here and Adam had an ex-wife. She came to the funeral, but left when I did. I think someone invited her to the wake, but I got the impression she wouldn't really have been welcome.'

'Oh?'

'Now, before you start reading anything into that, they divorced five years ago after ten years of marriage. No children and she's since remarried. Lived close on a hundred miles away and has a rock solid alibi for the night he died. I figure it's natural that the family might not want her there; equally natural, unless the divorce was really messy, that she'd want to say goodbye to someone she shared at least a decade with.' He paused. 'The father, Ernst, is an interesting man. Very strong, very proper. Looks like an old soldier.'

She laughed. 'What does an old soldier look like?'

'Oh, I don't know. Ramrod straight. That was the thing that struck me the first time we met and it struck me again today. I often wonder what happens to people like that if they have to bend.'

'Tough time, Christmas,' Naomi said thoughtfully. 'To lose family in any way. To have them die violently . . . must be even tougher.'

'Um, so it must be. It'll be tough on Clara too, the first year without her son and, from what I've seen, precious little family support elsewhere.'

'Hopefully she has friends.'

'Hopefully so, but having a killer for a son must put the dampner on your social life.'

'That's a callous way of putting it.'

'It's a truthful way, you know that.'

'Not if her friends are genuine,' Naomi objected.

62

Alec sighed. 'I suppose I'm feeling rather jaundiced,' he admitted. 'I wanted to be able to go there today and say, "Look, this is why Rob Beresford did what he did. It doesn't make it better or Adam any less dead, but at least you've got a reason." Instead, they were all terribly polite and very, very resentful. And frankly, I can't say I blame them. We had a good idea who the killer was the night it happened. It must seem to the family like we've done nothing since.'

'It hasn't really been that long,' Naomi objected. 'Two weeks, give or take. Frankly, they're lucky to have had the body released so soon.'

'I think the coroner pushed things through. Christmas and all that. You still fancy going out tonight or shall we get a film and a take away?'

'Add a nice bottle of wine and I'll settle for that. Why? Feeling lazy?'

'Hmm,' he kissed her again. 'Not exactly lazy, just not that sociable, if you know what I mean.'

She kissed him back. 'I've got a pretty good idea.'

'You wish that we would all go away?' Ernst asked her.

Jennifer was out on the staircase again. She didn't think anyone had noticed her slip away. 'Not you, Granddad,' she told him. 'I don't mind you being here.'

He seated himself one step down and handed her the second of the two glasses he was holding.

She took it uncertainly. 'I'm not supposed to drink wine. Not . . . you know.'

'While you are pregnant. Say it, Jen, there's no hiding it and you have to get used to the idea.'

'*I* am used to the idea. It's . . .'

He patted her hand. 'I know, I know. And that isn't wine, it's that fizzy grape stuff your mother likes.'

'Oh. OK, thanks then.' She placed it down beside her on the step.

Ernst peered at her over the rim of his own red wine. 'I was sorry you didn't come to the funeral.'

So that was it. Her parents had sent him out here to make her feel guilty. Guiltier, actually.

'Sorry,' he continued, 'but not surprised. Had I been able to find a good reason, I too would have stayed away.'

'You?' His accent was heavier tonight, she noted. Always there in the background and sometimes in the oddity of word order, it was more pronounced tonight, thickened by emotion. 'How could you have stayed away? Adam was . . .' She broke off and bit her lip.

'My son, yes. My child. As this,' he reached his hand and touched her, butterfly light, upon her belly. 'This is yours. A new life should not be hidden away.'

Jennifer's eyes filled with tears and she blinked them away, then wiped them on her sleeves when they insisted on pouring down her cheeks. 'That's not what they think,' she spat bitterly. 'Not them. All they can think about is how pissed off they are.'

Ernst shrugged. Never one to dress things off, he nodded. 'Yes, they are "pissed off" as you put it. They are disappointed too and a little shocked, especially because you will not say who. I think, if you had a boyfriend . . .?' He turned the last into a question and left it hanging in the air.

'You missed out "ashamed",' she snapped at him. She started to get up, wanting to retreat to her room and shut the door. Ernst reached out once more and took her hand.

'Sit down,' he said gently. 'I did not say "ashamed" because they are not ashamed. You are their child, as Adam was mine, as your mother is mine. They are shocked, yes, afraid for you, yes, but they and we all love you, Jennifer, and we will love your child when it arrives.' He sipped his wine, thoughtfully. 'One lost, one just beginning, that, I think, is the way of the world.'

His hand was shaking, Jennifer noticed. 'Do you hate him?' she asked. 'The one that did this?'

'That got you pregnant or killed my son?'

'I . . .' she realized with a shock that she didn't know. 'It's not the same thing, is it?'

'No, but both could be reasons to hate.' He hesitated. 'The . . . boy . . . who made you pregnant. Do you care for him? Does he know? Oh, I know, I know, you are sick to death of the questions. I won't ask them again. If he hurt you, left

64

you, then yes, I hate him. If you left him, if perhaps he doesn't know? Then no, I feel sorry for his loss.'

'His loss?'

'You don't tell him he has a son? That is loss.'

'It might be a girl.'

'Son, daughter, still a child. He or she. And the one who took my child? Of course I hate him. One day, if I ever understand, I might find it in my heart to forgive.'

'Mum will never forgive,' Jennifer said with absolute certainty.

'No, I don't think she will,' Ernst agreed. 'She and your uncle did not always see the world the same way. They often fought, even as children. That makes it worse for her.'

'How?'

'Because she has guilt too. Guilt that she might not have loved him enough when she still had the chance.'

'But that's stupid.'

'No, just human. Me, I have had a lifetime to get used to forgiveness. I have practice, you see. In time, if I understand the reasons, I might begin to forgive.'

Jennifer looked away. She couldn't think what to say. 'What if he had a reason,' she asked, finally, not looking at Ernst, but instead fixing her gaze upon the Christmas tree star. The tears had returned and the star fragmented into a thousand crystal shards. 'To kill someone. How big a reason would it have to be?'

Twelve

Clara had locked her doors and was about to go up to bed. The house still felt appallingly empty. *Clara* still felt appallingly empty and it could only get worse in the coming days.

She'd taken to avoiding town, anywhere she would be forced to confront the bright lights and artificial cheerfulness concurrent with the season. She and Rob had never made a big thing of Christmas, anyway. More often than not it had been just the two of them on the day, though, as Rob had got old enough to have his own social life, she had renewed old friendships and created the odd new one; made for herself a little round of parties and drinks and events that, for the past few years at least, had become traditional.

How long, she wondered in that random fashion her brain had tracked in these past weeks, how long does a pattern have to be established before you can classify it as tradition?

This year, anyway, this fragile custom had been broken. The invitations had materialized; some of them, anyway, but, she sensed, they had been half hearted and given in hope of her declining. She had become the ghost at the feast; the souvenir of mortality.

Clara was heading up the stairs when the doorbell rang. She checked the time on her watch. Just after eleven. Who on earth? Ignore it, she thought. Whoever it was, they had no right to be calling so late and in her experience only bad news came this late in the day. Resolute, she continued up the stairs, but whoever it was gave up on the bell and was banging upon the door. It seemed unlikely they would go away.

66

She returned to the hallway, trying to make out the shape she could just see through the obscure glass panel of the door. Should she call the police?

No doubt he could see her too. It looked, she decided, like a he. The banging increased in volume and insistence. She glanced at her watch again. He'd have the neighbours up and Steve next door was on earlies this week; that wasn't fair.

'Oh, for goodness sake!'

Putting the chain in place she opened the front door a crack. 'Who the hell do you think you are making that kind of noise? Do you know what time it is?'

The old man squared his shoulders and peered at her through the narrow gap. 'My name is Ernst Hensel,' he said. 'Your son killed mine.'

Clara had not, she decided, been in her right mind when she opened the door. Had some part of her, she wondered, been hoping he had been here looking for revenge? Would she have welcomed that?

Truthfully, Clara didn't know.

She had taken Ernst Hensel through to the kitchen, not into the living room as she would most guests, and she had told him to sit down in the chair Rob had settled in that night. Then, when the ordinary, normal things had been done, she had been at a loss, stood hovering in the doorway wondering what was expected. Was there etiquette for such moments?

Ernst seemed equally at a loss. He looked around at the tidy, nondescript kitchen with its bland beech effect cabinets and dark melamine worktops. At the shelves that housed her collection of blue and white plates. At the round table and spindle backed chairs and blue bowl, usually full of fruit but which was now home to only a single banana and an over-ripe pear. Clara looked where he looked, seeing, as though for the first time, as a stranger might, the chip showing white earthenware beneath the blue glaze, the mottled skin of fruit that, rightly, should have been binned days back. She caught the overripe smell of it, sickly sweet and verging on rot. She

67

noted the tidiness of the shelves and the lack of crockery in the drainer, signs that she had cooked only when hunger drove her to heat soup or make toast. She became aware, and wondered if he was aware too, that she had eaten properly only once or twice since Rob had died, and then only when someone else had, with forceful kindness, urged food upon her.

And finally, she looked upon the man himself, scrutinizing her as closely as she was him and with as much hostility. Or was it hostility? Looking into the cool grey eyes, slate grey set in a face that was itself grey with grief and weariness and crowned with a mane of hair, worn just that bit too long, that seemed to become more pallid even as she looked at it, she fancied there was no hostility. Just puzzlement.

'Why did you let me in?' he asked.

'I don't know. I suppose I was worried about the noise you were making.' She grimaced, aware of how odd that must sound. 'I was worried what the neighbours might think. Why did you come here?'

Ernst Hensel nodded slowly as though considering the question. 'I came,' he said, 'because, today, I buried my son. I wanted to see for myself what kind of woman could give birth to such a creature that might take his life away.'

Thirteen

'What did you talk about?' Patrick was awed and aware that the others felt the same. The idea that Clara and the father of the victim should meet, should talk, was an outrageous one.

'How did he find out where you lived?' Becky demanded. 'Did the police tell him? They had no right!'

Clara shook her head. 'No, he says he followed me home from the funeral. From Rob's funeral. He said he had no idea why, just the need to know. He'd figured out from the news reports and odd things the police let slip that Rob had to be the one and he wanted to confront me at the funeral, but then, when he got there it seemed inhumane.'

'Inhumane! Coming here was bloody inhumane.' Charlie couldn't get to grips with the idea. 'He was too fucking scared to come out and say anything at the funeral with all of us there, so he came round when he knew you'd be on your own. You've done nothing. It's all wrong. All fucking wrong.'

Clara leaned across the table and, briefly, touched his hand. 'It's all right,' she said. 'In a strange kind of way, I'm glad he did. And I'm glad you all came over tonight, but shouldn't you be with your families?' It was, after all, Christmas Eve.

The glances they exchanged were puzzled, embarrassed. 'Mum and *him* have gone out for the evening,' Becky said finally.

'Mine are at my uncle's, then they'll go to Mass,' Charlie admitted. 'I said I'd maybe join them later. Mam is a bit funny about it, you know. She doesn't bother any other time, just Christmas and Easter.'

Patrick said nothing. He was supposed to be with his dad and Mari, but when Becky had phoned, felt it more important to be with his friends and come to see Clara.

'I might not have been here,' Clara said gently. 'I might have been out.'

Another awkward glance. It had not occurred to any of them that she had places to go or maybe people to be with.

'I'm sorry,' Becky said. 'If you were going out?'

Clara's shoulders slumped. 'Oh, who am I kidding,' she said. 'No, I'd no plans. Friends invited me over, but, frankly, I think I'd have been a right wet blanket. I'm sure they were relieved when I said no.'

'I'll be glad when it's all over,' Becky said feelingly. 'I never thought I'd hate Christmas. You know, when you're a little kid and you wait all year for your birthday and then for Christmas and it's all bright lights and pressies and your mam spoiling you . . .' She trailed off, blinking rapidly. Tears were still rarely far away.

'But what did you talk about?' Patrick asked again. He'd heard Alec and Naomi discuss something called restorative justice – was that the right phrase? When victims of burglaries meet with the housebreaker. It was supposed to help everyone see the other point of view and stop re-offending. Patrick was dubious, but, even if that worked, it seemed a world away from what Ernst Hensel had done.

'We talked about them,' Clara said. 'We talked about *them*.'

'My son is a murderer.

'It's hard for anyone to comprehend what that means. Half the time, I don't understand it myself, but it's a truth that wakes me in the middle of the night and one that creeps up on me when I'm doing the most trivial of things like cleaning windows or walking to the shops.

'My child killed a man.'

'He killed my boy,' he said. 'I know exactly what this means.'

She drew a deep, sharp breath and held it, nodded before exhaling with a painful gasp. 'Why did you come here?'

'I told you. I'm sorry for what I said. It was . . . unkind.'

'Unkind!' She was at a loss. Unkind seemed such an insipid, passive word. 'You accused me of being a monster. A monster that brought something far worse into the world. That's more than unkind.'

His gaze found and held hers and he reached out, halfway across the table as though he might take her hand. 'Can you blame me?'

She hesitated, then shook her head. A rapid little gesture as though she had to force the movement. 'No.'

The stranger – his face drawn and grey as though he suffered from a long traumatic illness – leaned back in his chair. That same chair . . . For a moment she could see Rob's face and lanky body superimposed over that of this older man. This pained and grieving man.

'I've lived with it,' he said. 'I've rehearsed, almost every day since it happened. First, I thought of what I would say to his killer when I saw him. What I might do. In the beginning, all I could think was that I should find some way of getting him alone. I would hide a knife in the sleeve of my coat and, once I had him there, I'd stab him once in the heart, just like he stabbed my son . . .'

'Don't. Please.' She rose abruptly from the table, but seemed unable to move further. Instead, she clutched the edge of it until her knuckles whitened.

He seemed not to hear.

'Then I found out that the killer too was dead and I knew I'd have to find another way. I rehearsed what I'd say to you over and over again. I was certain; I would look into your face and see the eyes of my enemy. That I would look at you and recognize what it was that made your son kill mine and I would understand.'

'And do you?' Her voice was shrill and thin. An anguished bird shriek that caused him to lift his gaze from the table top and stare once more into her face.

He shook his head.

'I saw bewilderment,' he said. 'I see a woman who has lost her child and I'm sorry for what I said. I tried to keep quiet, but, you understand, I spent all these days rehearsing . . . something. I had to say the words.'

71

She sat down again, heavily, as though the last strength deserted her. 'I should never have let you in. I should have shut the door and called the police.'

'Why didn't you?' His voice, gentle now, curious.

'I don't know. Maybe . . . maybe there was a part of me hoped you had that knife hidden in your sleeve.'

He smiled sadly, and shrugged out of his coat. 'See,' he said, turning back the cuff. 'I even opened the lining and I stitched a little channel ready for the hiding of it.'

The hiding of it.

She'd been aware of his accent. His English was perfect apart from the slight and occasional change in syntax that was so very foreign. 'Did you? Hide the knife?'

He shook his head. 'My stitching is poor,' he told her with a sad smile that still, somehow, touched his eyes. 'The channel I stitched, it tore and frayed the lining.' He turned the cuff back further so she could see the strained fabric and the inch long tear. 'But I searched, trying to find a blade that would be the exact fit. I searched the hardware shops and the markets and those odd little places that sell black clothes and ornamental daggers. Goths, I think they call themselves. The young people who wear black and paint their faces white. I searched, because it gave me purpose. We all must have purpose. Some way of relief.

'My daughter,' he shrugged, 'she cleaned her house. She scrubbed the walls until they bled.'

'Daughter? He . . . he had a sister?' Even now, she couldn't say his name.

'He had a sister. Beth. She is called Elizabeth. She is thirty-eight. Adam was forty-three.'

Adam. He had a name. She knew it. She ought to use it, but she still could not. Instead, she said softly, 'My son was just seventeen.'

'We talked about our children,' Clara continued. 'About the loss we felt and the way he had wanted revenge, then realized that even that was useless.'

'He might have hurt you.' Becky couldn't keep the shock or the fear from her voice. 'Clara, you should never have let him in. Promise us, you won't do anything like that again.'

Clara smiled, amused and touched by this sudden role reversal.

'I mean it,' Becky continued earnestly. 'Clara, you have to be careful.'

'She's right,' Charlie emphasized. 'Sounds to me like he's a picnic short of a sandwich.'

Shouldn't that be sandwich short of a picnic? Patrick wondered, but to correct seemed picky in the present context. Another time, another place and Charlie's mistake would have been shredded, kept them amused for ages. 'What are you doing tomorrow?' he asked. 'You could come to us. Dad and Mari won't mind.'

'Mari?'

'My nan,' Patrick explained.

Clara smiled at him and shook her head. 'It's kind of you,' she said. 'But I really couldn't impose. Christmas is a family time and, like I said, I don't think my company would be very good.'

'OK, then,' Charlie said slowly. 'But we're all going to ring you. OK?'

'OK, then, thank you,' Clara said. Then it struck her. 'You think I might do something . . . like Rob did, don't you?'

Again, the exchanged glances, the awkward shuffling and Clara bit down the urge to laugh. It seemed both touching and absurd that these three, young enough to be her kids . . .

Like Rob had been. The urge to laugh receded, died. 'Charlie,' she said softly. 'I'll be honest. I've thought about it. In the days after Rob . . . died . . . I could think of nothing else. Life didn't seem to have much point. But I've got this far. I'm still here and, now, it seems like I'd be letting Rob down by letting go. You understand that?'

They nodded, though she could see they were unconvinced. But Clara meant every word. She now had a reason to go on and, ironically, that reason had been provided by Ernst Hensel.

*   *   *

73

'The police will do nothing more,' he told her. 'The nice detective, he came to the funeral and I asked him, "Do you know why my son died?" He could tell me no more than that first day. A single stab wound to the heart, made by the knife I had given him so many years ago I do not recall. They will close the file, put it away in a cabinet and from time to time, someone will take it out, read the words and shake their heads in sadness before putting it away. That, I know, is all the police will do.'

'And you want more.' Clara wanted more.

'I need more,' Ernst emphasized. 'Alone, what can I do? Together, it seems to me, we may see more, know more.' He waited, drawing back from her but keeping his eyes fixed upon her face. He shrugged back into his overcoat, but still he waited until, finally, Clara nodded. She heard him sigh.

'I did not come here intending to ask such a thing,' he said softly. 'But I cannot live on and do nothing. I will die of this nothing.'

'We're going to find out what went on that night,' Clara told them. 'However bad it is, we just can't go on without knowing what went wrong.'

Patrick and the others had spent another hour with Clara, covering old ground, it seemed to him, analyzing what she told them about Ernst. Coming back to the letter Rob was supposed to have found and which Clara still could not understand.

'Did he actually say it was a letter?' she asked finally.

'I think so, that's what you said, isn't it, Becks?'

Becky frowned, thinking hard. She shook her head. 'He was pissed,' she said, casting an apologetic look at Clara. 'Really, really pissed. I made him drink about a gallon of coffee before I let him walk home. He said he'd found some-thing and read it. Something he'd found when you were out one day. He'd . . . he'd been looking for anything that might tell him who his dad was and he was just boiling over, mad, because he . . . Clara, he said you'd been lying to him. Given him the wrong name or something.

74

'I asked him how he knew and he said he'd found something, read it. I guess I just thought it must be a letter, you know.'

Clara nodded but could still shed no light. 'The police didn't discover anything.'

'Would they know what to look for?' Patrick asked. 'I mean, anyway, they'd be looking for anything that might explain why he killed that man, not about looking for his dad, even if there was a connection, they might not be able to see it because they don't know the background.'

'You're probably right,' Clara said. She rubbed her eyes with the palms of her hands, suddenly very weary. 'It's late,' she said. 'And, frankly, I'm knackered and you lot should be getting home.'

They shuffled their chairs back, got to their feet. 'OK,' Charlie said. 'But we'll ring tomorrow and we want to know anything you do with that man, right?'

Clara smiled weakly and promised to keep them informed. She watched from the door as they wandered off towards town and home. She felt utterly drained.

'I don't like it,' Charlie said. 'He could be any kind of maniac.'

'You should tell Alec,' Becky was adamant. 'The police should know.'

Patrick nodded. 'I'll be seeing him tomorrow,' he said. He glanced at his watch. 'Shit. Later today. It's gone one. I was supposed to be home this evening. Dad makes this big thing about Christmas Eve.' Previous years, so had Patrick, giving in to the childish impulses he had so enjoyed in his younger days. One present had always been allowed on Christmas Eve and, even though he knew pretty much what he'd be getting these days, there was still something childishly special about choosing the package from beneath the tree and going off to bed with that frisson of further expectation.

More than that though, it was part of feeling loved and safe and, suddenly, plaintively, Patrick craved that feeling, was eager for home. He left Charlie and Becky by the tow

75

path. They lived only a street apart; Patrick a quarter mile the other way. Once on the tow path, he began to run, feeling somehow as though all the ghosts he had collected in his seventeen years of life were at his heels.

Fourteen

There was a light on in the living room. Other than that the house was in darkness.

Patrick checked the time. It was getting on for one fifteen. He let himself in and thought about going straight upstairs to his room, even though he knew that would just make things worse in the morning. His moment of indecision took that option away. Harry appeared in the doorway, standing in the patch of light that spilled out into the darkened hall. Patrick, used now to the darkness, blinked at the brilliance of it.

'I've taken your grandmother home,' Harry said.

Grandmother. Harry never called Mari that on any but the most formal of occasions. Mari hated it. Patrick called her Nan or even Mari but never Grandmother. Patrick knew now, had he been in any doubt before, that he was in deep trouble.

'I'm sorry, Dad.' Apologize straight away. He'd soon cool down.

Wrong.

'I tried to phone you. We waited. We worried, Patrick. We even phoned the hospitals . . .'

'You did what? Why?'

'Because I didn't think you'd willingly stay out, not when you'd promised to be back. If you'd called, it wouldn't have been so bad.'

'I'm sorry, Dad. I had stuff to do.'

'What stuff? Dammit, Patrick, it was Christmas Eve. You used to love Christmas Eve.'

'I still do, I . . .' Anger surged taking Patrick by surprise. It wasn't aimed at his dad, not really, but it boiled and bubbled from him and Harry got scalded anyway. 'Dad, I'm

77

not a kid anymore. I'm seventeen. I had other stuff to do tonight. Anyone would think I'd committed a bloody crime the way you go on. I just went out, that's all. I was with my friends, all right? Maybe I didn't want to be stuck in with you and Nan, ever thought of that?'

He made to go up the stairs, but Harry blocked his way.

'No, not all right. What the hell makes you think you can talk to me like that, treat us like that? Since you think so little of us I'm surprised you bothered to come back at all. Why don't you just get back out there with your so-called friends?'

'Fine then, I will.' Patrick wheeled around and headed back for the door. Any second now, he thought, he'll call me back. He won't say sorry and neither will I, but we'll make some tea and talk about nothing and in the morning it'll be forgotten. He paused with his hand on the front door, but no sound came from Harry. No sign of a reprieve. 'Fine,' Patrick shouted and pulled the door open, then slammed it behind him.

In the hall, Harry's shoulders slumped. He had missed his cue. Deliberately?

'Patrick,' he said. Then shouted at the door, 'Patrick!' But the barrier was now in place and by the time he reached the entrance and looked up and down the street, there was no sign of his son.

'Harry, what the hell?' Alec had pulled on a pair of jeans and Naomi appeared in the background fastening the tie on her robe. 'What's happened, what's wrong?'

'Is he here? Patrick, did he come here?'

'Patrick? No, what makes you think? God's sake, you're shaking like a leaf, are you sick? What's going on?'

Harry allowed Alec to sit him down. Napoleon whined anxiously and nuzzled at his hand. 'Patrick ran out on me,' he said. 'We had a stupid argument and he ran off. Alec, I told him to go.'

'OK, now start at the start and we'll sort it out.'

'Shall I make some tea?' Naomi asked.

'No. No, thank you. I've got to get out again. Look for him.'

'You've got to sit down and wait while we get dressed,' Alec told him. 'Then we'll all go. You're in no fit state to drive. Have you been drinking?'

'I . . . Oh God, Alec I don't know. I had a couple with Mari, then a couple more while I was waiting for Patrick to turn up. I . . .'

'OK, lucky you didn't get pulled over. Now, sit tight.'

Harry waited impatiently while they dressed and then they bundled into Alec's car, Napoleon grumbling at being left behind in the flat.

Where would he go? Harry couldn't think. For a while they drove aimlessly, Harry knowing approximately where Charlie and Becky lived but not the exact address. It was Naomi who finally had the brain wave.

'The canal,' she said. 'He goes down there to think.'

'The canal?' She heard the sudden panic in Harry's voice and wished she'd kept her mouth shut. 'This time of the morning. It's not safe down there any time. He's got no right.'

No right to do what? Naomi wondered. To scare Harry like this? Or to put himself in danger. Maybe they were one and the same. 'It's OK, Harry. We'll find him. Alec, if you drive towards the marina, you can see back along a good length.'

'Already on my way,' Alec told her. Then, 'Harry, that looks like him, standing on the bridge.'

Which bridge, Naomi thought. The one Rob jumped from?

Alec stopped the car and Harry was out before he cut the engine, running towards the footbridge and calling Patrick's name.

Fifteen

Christmas morning was a subdued affair. Patrick *felt* as though he had a hangover even though he'd imbibed no alcohol, and Harry probably really did. He drove the mile or so to his mother's house with overweening care and winced when Patrick slammed the door.

Mari took one look at their faces and Patrick could see her make the decision not to lecture or even ask for an explanation. Instead, she hugged him hard; strong beyond belief for such a small woman, she almost knocked the breath from him. Then hugged her son too and ushered them inside.

Mari's living room was always cramped. Oversized sofas and a large TV filled the available space. Christmas saw the addition of a massive tree, piled and festooned with ornaments that had been around since her own children were tiny. This largesse was added to every year until the green branches were almost hidden beneath the festival of red and gold and purple and blue. Mari bought what she fancied. Co-ordination was something they did on television make-over programmes. Nice to look at, but not for her.

Parcels wrapped in garish paper filled what little space was left beneath the tree and spread out on to the hearth rug, dangerously close to the fire. The room was a little too warm, but today, Patrick didn't mind. He had felt chilled ever since his dad had found him on the bridge. Chilled and shivery as though coming down with the flu, though he figured viruses had nothing to do with it.

The door bell rang again just as he flopped down in the chair next to the tree. Naomi and Alec's voices reached him. He was glad they were here; it diluted the attention that might otherwise be directed his way. His dad hovered in the doorway, glancing anxiously in Patrick's direction and then turning expectantly to greet their friends.

He should tell her how he feels, Patrick thought suddenly. Tell her to ditch Alec and move in with him. It was, he recognized, a pretty silly thought. Naomi was probably in no doubt about the depth of Harry's feelings, but she'd made her choice and gone for handsome rather than blandly dependable. Not, Patrick admitted, that he'd anything against Alec. He liked him a lot and then there'd be that weirdness of having Naomi as his step-mother. Patrick wasn't really sure either of them could handle that.

His reverie was interrupted by Naomi bending to kiss him on the cheek. 'You OK?' she asked under her breath.

'Yeah.' He kissed her back. 'It's all right, thanks.'

'Good.' She straightened up and turned back to talk to Mari. 'Mum says to thank you for the brooch, she loves it.'

'Oh, she's welcome. I'm looking forward to seeing her tomorrow. It'll be lovely getting us all together.'

Patrick groaned inwardly. Oh yes, the gathering of the Blake and Jones clans and anyone else counted as family. He was glad it wasn't happening here, at Mari's; hard enough to cram the five of them in as it was. Alec's family, he knew, lived quite a distance away, which simplified that, he supposed. He thought of the other part of his own family, his mum and step-father and step-brothers over in the States. They'd be phoning later, and just for the merest instant he thought how much better it might have been had he gone there for the celebrations.

Then he caught sight of his dad, looking at him with that intense expression on his face that Patrick vaguely recognized as love and he knew he'd rather be here and, more to the point, that he should be making an effort of some sort.

Awkwardly, Patrick got up and went over to Harry. 'I'm sorry,' he mumbled.

'So am I.' Harry said. 'Now, let it go, eh?'

Patrick nodded and relaxed, just a little, switched his attention to Mari, the apron-clad Father Christmas, struggling to fetch the stack of parcels out from beneath the tree.

*   *   *

81

Jennifer tried not to mind that a lot of the presents seemed to have considered the baby rather than her. It was kind of Great-Aunt Sheila to have knitted and Uncle Joe's toys meant for a one-year-old were well meaning. Even her parents seemed determined to get in on the act, unveiling the combination baby buggy come car seat with all the ceremony with which they might have revealed a rocking horse or a new bike in the years before.

Sure, they'd also got her some CDs she wanted and there was the promise of a shopping trip to get new clothes after the baby arrived, but it all felt a little flat.

Uncle Adam would have found her something special, Jenny thought and the idea brought fresh tears flooding to her eyes. He always did, managing to find something unusual or beautiful or just plain weird. One year it had been an antique bracelet decorated with blue enamel flowers. Another, a music box with a marquetry lid. Last year a locket, large and silver, heavily engraved and inside pictures of a Victorian couple and a lock of hair.

Her mother had found it macabre not to say unsuitable, but Jennifer had been enchanted. Who were they? What happened to them? Was this to commemorate their wedding day?

This year there would be no special gift, no stolen moments sitting on the stairs to chat, no laughing Christmas kiss beneath the mistletoe in the hall – no mistletoe anyway this year – no Uncle Adam.

She tried to smile, to thank everyone, to nod gratefully at the advice and the demonstrations – look, I've put these little bow buttons on the cardi . . . the seat lifts off like this so it goes straight into the car . . . the little train makes five different noises when you press the different buttons. Very educational, but it was hard. Suddenly, she was being treated as an *almost* adult. A not very intelligent one, having to be given loads of support, special needs kind of adult, but an adult of sorts just the same. Jen found herself thinking she would have given anything just to be five years old again. Just, even, to have set the clock back five months or so and to know how not to be so stupid this time around.

Grandfather Ernst saved his gift until last and then slipped a small box into her hand. She was puzzled. Granddad always gave her money, telling her he never knew what to buy and the card, with its usual cash gift had already been supplied. She opened the box. 'Oh. But this was Grammer's.'

Ernst nodded. 'She always wanted that it should be yours.'

Her mother came over to see. Jen saw her expression change from one of mild interest to one of pain. 'Dad, this was mother's ring. Her *wedding* ring.'

'And I gave *you* the engagement ring, Beth. She intended always that this should go to Jennifer.'

'Yes, sure, but for when she . . .'

Married, Jennifer supplied. For when she got married. Not for now. It was a very simple ring, narrow and plain and worn but with three tiny chips of diamond set at equal distance round the band. Jennifer had always loved it. 'Thank you,' she told Ernst, but she didn't know what felt worse, receiving the ring now, at such a wrong and disappointing time or seeing in her mother's eyes just how much she felt that Jennifer had let them down.

Clara had never spent this day alone but she was surprised by how little she minded after all. It was as though Christmas, normally a time of such over the top celebration, as she tried to make up to Rob for the lack of family and lack of other people's gifts, had simply failed to happen this year.

She watched the television, she reminded herself to eat and even cooked a proper meal – pasta rather than turkey and all the trimmings, but it was still better than she had been doing. She dozed in the chair and ignored the world. Charlie's promised phone call, closely followed by Becky's, took her by surprise. Both were brief, but genuinely caring and some part of her that she allowed to feel was grateful. 'Patrick probably won't call until later,' Charlie told her. 'He has to keep the line clear for his mam to phone from Florida.'

'Florida?'

'Yeah, she got married again, lives over there.'

'Oh, I see. Thanks, Charlie.' She finished the call and put down the phone, suddenly surprised at how little she actually knew about these three youngsters who had taken her under their collective wing.

Rob, she thought, had chosen his friends well. Or, at least some of them. Her thoughts drifted to Ernst Hensel and she wondered what he was doing today and if he was allowing himself, as she was not, to miss his son.

Sixteen

New Year's day. It always felt like you should make a special effort to do something different, Naomi thought. She wasn't one for resolutions – the longest she'd ever kept one was about a week – but she did like using the day to make plans.

She and Alec had been to a party the night before. He'd been lucky this year, not on the rota for either Christmas day or New Year's Eve. She couldn't recall the last time that had happened. Both were now feeling the effects of the night before and Alec suggested a walk by the sea to clear their collective heads and give Napoleon a proper run. The dog loved the shingle beach. They'd left his harness at home, putting him on the lead so he knew this was time off. Once she felt the stones crunching beneath her boots, Naomi bent to unhook the lead. She laughed, as with an excited yip, Napoleon raced off to snap at the breaking waves.

'He's trying to eat the foam,' Alec said. 'Do you think it will do him any harm?'

'If he can survive eating the bits of bacon you've carried around in your pocket all day, I'm sure he'll be OK with a bit of salt water.' Naomi said.

'Left-overs,' Alec said. 'Always seems such a waste to throw them away.'

'And, of course, you don't order a bit extra just so you *have* some left-overs.'

'I might. I also accept donations. Napoleon's a popular fellow.'

'I don't think I want to know.' She clasped Alec's arm securely, still a little wary of the uneven surface and turned her face into the blustery, salt tanged wind. She could feel it roughening her cheeks and blowing her shoulder length hair into utter disarray. She imagined that it blew as hard through her thoughts, taking away all the dead and dried and empty stuff like so many decaying leaves, sweeping her mind clean.

'We should set a date,' Alec said, interrupting her spring cleaning.

'A date? For what?'

'For the wedding, of course. You don't think I'm going to let you go through another year as a single woman, do you?'

Naomi laughed. 'And why not?'

'Because,' he said seriously, turning her to face him. 'Because I have this horrible fear that you might still get away.'

Even before they had a grave to visit, Mari and Harry Jones had made the New Year pilgrimage to lay flowers for Helen. Patrick had accompanied them the past three years and he came this year too, laden with flowers as Mari linked her arm through her son's and walked a little ahead. They chatted softly and they walked slowly, pausing now and then to admire a pile of tributes or acknowledge the grave of someone they knew. Or Mari knew. Mari, Patrick thought ruefully, seemed to have something to say about just about everyone laid to rest here. Patrick, arms filled with roses and lilies, didn't join the conversation. This, he had always sensed, was their time and, though he was welcome, this visit represented a shared past he knew only in the most storylike of ways. Aunt Helen as she would have been was, for Patrick, a ghost at every feast, though a benign one. For his father and Nan, she was solid flesh and blood with all the sensory reminders that brought. She laughed, she talked, she argued, she hugged and played with toys. She had opinions and cried when her hamster died.

Rob, Patrick reminded himself had been flesh and blood too. He thought about his friend, the sudden burst of laughter, the rages, swiftly kindled and as swiftly damped. The love of cars – which Patrick didn't share – and graphic novels –

which Patrick did. The trip to the cinema to see the Frank
Miller film, Patrick sneaking in with the others, horribly
aware that he couldn't really pass for eighteen. Rob, who
had looked older than that forever, buying the tickets and
hoping no one asked for identification.

Rob and Becky. Becky loved him far more than he loved
her, Patrick knew that. He knew it because *he* cared more
for Rob than Rob was capable of giving back and he recognized the signs. It wasn't, he thought, that Rob was shallow
or uncaring, simply that Rob was one of those people who
always seemed to glide upon the surface of life whereas he,
Patrick, spent all his time struggling to learn how to doggy
paddle. Surface tension both supported his friend and
prevented him from glimpsing life below.

Or it had done.

It must, Patrick thought, be like being vaccinated and
building an immunity to illness. Having to struggle and fight
meant you were used to the shock of reality. Until recently,
Patrick sensed, Rob had been able to hold out against reality
by skimming lightly like a pond skater. Then, when something beneath had grabbed a leg and he had been forced to
fight to stay on top, he had, inevitably, been dragged down
and down; unpractised at the skills which might have kept
him floating. Patrick still didn't know *what* it was that had
grabbed him but it had drowned him both figuratively and
literally.

Patrick had spent some time drawing last night. A surprise
gift from Harry had been the ultra expensive marker pens
Patrick had been buying one at a time as he could afford
them. Harry had bought him a pack of twelve in the grey
scale range and, better still, the refill ink for the shades he
used most often. Patrick saw Naomi's hand in this. She'd
probably guided Harry through the internet ordering – the
sets weren't available anywhere locally – and also told him
what paper Patrick required. Last night, Patrick had started
to draw and inevitably, his drawings had featured Rob. In
graphic tones, he had depicted his friend standing on the
bridge, falling into the still, dark water that flowed beneath,
visualized him, caught up in the weeds and dragged down

by the debris that choked the canal. The life ebbing from him as he gave up the fight to skate upon the surface.

Patrick had poured his emotions into the work, turning it, at the same time, into a story at one remove from himself and as a cathartic exercise.

He wondered what Harry would make of the pictures. What his counsellor would say. Patrick allowed himself an inner laugh at that. She'd be so busy rationalizing it, she'd probably miss the point.

What point was that?

The point that he missed his friend. That he felt as though a part of him had drowned alongside Rob and that this was the only way he could even start to think about letting go.

Patrick looked down at the path, blinking back tears. The tarmac had been roughly embedded with gravel, intended to aid drainage, but the job had been badly done and it chipped and shredded at the surface. Patrick scuffed his feet at the loosened stones, watching the way the runnels from the recent shower of rain trailed away like a miniature river in a landscape of mountainous gravel.

One thing he had learnt from his drawings last night: he wanted someone to blame for all the stuff that had happened, but there was no one to whom blame seemed to apply. The other thing was that he was mad as hell at his friend. Rob, Patrick felt, had gone away, run away, left them all high and dry like the gravel on the path, stranded on their stony little islands and all they could do was shout across at one another, separated from the rest of the world and even from each other because they didn't know the reason why.

'We're here Patrick,' Mari said, taking the flowers from his arms. She smiled, then looked into his flushed face and asked softly, 'Are you all right?'

'Yeah, I'm fine. No really. I'm fine.'

Harry seemed about to add his voice to the questions, but Mari drew him away and Patrick was grateful for her understanding. He watched as they bent to arrange flowers on the grave and wondered if they were ever angry with Helen, as

88

unreasonably angry as he was with Rob, that she had never even said goodbye.

It was only because of Ernst that Clara was able to go to the place where her son had died. He arrived, unannounced mid morning and told her to get her coat, they were going out. He had flowers in the car. Flowers for her and for himself.

'It seemed right,' he said when she asked him why.

They drove first to the site of his own child's murder. Clara sat beside him, conscious of the surreal, the impossibly bizarre aspect to all this.

'What do your family think?' she asked. She didn't need to elucidate.

'They don't know, yet, that I am seeing you. I will tell, but not today. Today, my daughter sleeps late and Denny, her husband, will have taken himself fishing. Jennifer . . . I do not know what Jennifer will do.'

'Your granddaughter? How old is she?'

'Seventeen, the same age as your boy. She is pregnant.'

'Oh.'

'Yes, oh. But what is done . . . She upsets her mother because she will not name the father. For myself, I think she feels shame. He was someone she would rather not have known. We do not always make love wisely when we are seventeen.'

Clara laughed. 'No,' she said. 'No we certainly do not. Though, I never regretted Rob. He was . . . loving, funny, clever, everything I could have wanted in a son.' She bit her lip, wondering if she had hurt this man's feelings. She looked for distraction. 'When is she due?'

'April. Early April. I hope it will be a girl.'

They fell silent then and Clara looked out of the window at unfamiliar streets. Her home town, but a part she did not know well. Big houses, some turned into expensive flats, some still family homes, lined a broad tree-lined road. Ernst pulled into one of the side streets and parked.

'It was here?'

'It was here.'

He came round and opened the door. Clara got out. The

houses, she thought, must be Edwardian. They were only a ten minute walk from the promenade. A privet hedge surrounded the corner house, almost hiding the wide, square windows and, glimpsed through the wrought iron gate, what she recognized by the spreading shape as a magnolia tree, stretched protectively across the front lawn.

'The people in that building, they heard him shout and looked out. At first, they could see nothing. Then they heard steps running and came to look. Adam was already good as dead.

'The man gave chase, but he did not see which way the attacker had gone. I think he must have recognized that Adam had been stabbed and was afraid of a man with a knife. I do not imagine he ran too fast. I would not have run too fast.'

'Wouldn't you?' Somehow, she thought Ernst would have done, he would have pursued no matter what the threat. She had noted the way he turned his story into just that; a story. Not mentioning Rob by name.

'You are an unusual man,' she said softly. 'I don't think I understand you.'

'Madam,' he said with sudden odd formality. 'I do not think I understand myself.'

He laid his flowers beside the road sign and stepped back, head bowed, his lips moving as though he prayed. Clara fancied that instead of prayer, he talked to the dead, head tilted as though waiting for a reply.

'Do you hate me still?' Clara asked him as they moved back towards the car.

He nodded. 'A little part of me, yes. But mostly, I pity you.' He paused mid step and turned towards her, laying a hand gently on her arm. 'But I still hate your son. Can you forgive me for that?'

Numbly, slipping back into that surreal land she had been moving through since she got into his car, Clara nodded. 'I can understand that. Can you understand that I feel that way too, no matter how irrational and cruel that may sound? I hate your son for whatever he did to make mine . . . do what he did. I know Rob, Rob was gentle, kind, yes, he had a

90

temper, but when he lost it . . . it was because he believed he was righteously angry. Ernst, your son must have done something to precipitate this.'

He did not reply. Instead, he moved back to the car and opened the door. Unthinking, Clara slid into the seat. It was only as they drove away that two things occurred to her that struck her as odd. One, easily dismissed, was that it was strange he should come here and not go to Adam's grave. The second, stranger still the more she pondered on it was that, despite Clara describing her son, defending him and Ernst telling her about his family, he had said nothing about Adam. No description; no defence. No fatherly comments beyond the expression of his love and even that had been tacit.

'Were you close to him?' The question had to be asked.

Ernst glanced at her then fixed his gaze back on to the road. His hands tightened on the steering wheel. 'I thought we were,' he said. 'Then, I realized that we had grown lazy over time. We said only the expected things; discussed only those topics about which we could guess the other's opinion. I knew what my son was, years ago, before he moved on to live his own life and I took back mine. After that, I think we both forgot that the other might change and grow.'

'That's sad,' Clara said.

'Yes,' Ernst agreed. 'As sad as you not knowing what your son might have come to be.'

Jennifer had printed out a street map from the internet but even so it was hard to find the bridge. She'd walked from the middle of town, buses being sparse on the holiday and her feet ached. So did her back. The baby seemed to have caught her mood. It was restless and fidgety. She still couldn't get used to feeling it move. It was at the one time wonderful and horrifying. An alien thing growing inside her. Occasionally she felt a jolt of euphoric love; more often just a rising panic.

She hadn't bothered with a bag, just stuffed some money and the map into the pocket of her coat. In the other pocket was a clipping from the evening paper. She slipped it out, furtive and half ashamed, looked at the picture. Rob Beresford stared back at her with embarrassed eyes, the prize he'd won – and the cause of his embarrassment – clutched between his hands.

The bridge had once been for traffic but more recently had been closed to all but bikes and walkers. Cast iron bollards keeping the traffic away. Jen paused on the opposite side of the road. There was someone already there, at her intended destination. A boy with red hair and a girl about her own age. They stood close together, hunched against the cold. The girl had red roses clutched between her hands. As Jennifer watched, she dropped the roses over the balustrade.

Jennifer looked away. It seemed suddenly stupid to be here. Turning on her heel, Jennifer walked angrily, back the way she'd come.

Seventeen

Ernst stayed over at his daughter's house two or three times a month. This was a hangover from the time he had been the main babysitter for Jennifer and the guest room was often referred to as Grandpa's room.

Lisle, his wife had died of cancer some ten years before and the family had clung tight for a time, Ernst practically living in the spare room, unable to face the return to an empty house and his daughter, Beth, knocked sideways by the death of a mother she – and her husband for that matter – had adored.

Adam, Ernst thought, had gone through the motions of grief, and Ernst was equitable enough to believe him to have been sincere, but he had soon drifted out of the family circle once again, picked up his own life and moved along.

At the time, it had seemed natural; Ernst regretted it now.

The room was warm and quiet, a fire burning in the grate adding its friendly crackle to the close drawn curtains and the soft light. Music played, Jennifer's choice, a male singer Ernst quite liked despite his lack of musical range. David something, Jennifer had said, adding that she liked his lyrics but the volume had been turned low enough not to interrupt their conversation and Ernst could not judge. Childhood evening spent together, she might have pestered him to play chess, a game he had taught her to play, as she grew older he'd be presented with homework garnished with pleas for help he was sure she did not need. It was his attention she craved, not his expertise.

Tonight, parents out visiting friends and the two of them left alone, she sat with a blanket spread across her lap and a mug of hot coffee clasped between her hands, staring at the fire.

Ernst, busy with his own thoughts, left Jennifer to hers, sensing she was building up to something important and that she needed time. He gazed fondly at the long fair hair, shining with red notes in the fire light, the pale skin, always pale even in a hot, dry summer. The dark eyes that seemed at odd with the otherwise fragile colouring. Lisle's eyes, he thought. Years ago, he had fallen in love with those eyes.

'Did you have a good day?' he asked at last. 'Beth said you were out for most of it.'

'Did she want you to find out where I'd gone?'

'She didn't say. I think she was relieved you had gone out. You have been something of a recluse, my love.'

'Yeah, well. It's hard. People stare.'

'Perhaps not as much as you might think. People, I have found, think only of their own lives most of the time.'

She shrugged, her mouth turned down.

He sipped his wine.

'Granddad, do you think I'm going to love this baby?'

He considered. 'Most mothers do. I suppose instinct teaches you to love.'

'Did you love Mum and Uncle Adam straight away?'

Ernst smiled. 'Oh yes,' he said. 'But I freely admit I was terrified as well, especially the first time. There he was, this perfect, tiny person, screaming loud enough to shake the walls of Jericho and yes, I loved him.'

'I think I'll just be terrified.'

'Perhaps, at first.'

'But isn't that bad? I mean, how can I be a good mother if I'm just scared?'

Ernst laughed softly. 'Darling, I think it is the fear that makes us good parents, not the lack of it. The desire to protect.' He looked quizzically over the rim of his glass. 'Do you love the baby now?'

Jennifer shrugged. 'Sometimes.'

'Sometimes is a beginning. And –' he hesitated – 'the father. Did you love him sometimes?'

He had trespassed. For a moment he thought she might get up and walk out of the room, but she just clutched the coffee mug more tightly and looked away.

'I never loved him,' she said at last. 'Not even sometimes.'

'Then I am doubly sorry for you.'

'Doubly?' Her look accused.

'Because, my darling, for one thing, you have to endure this alone and far too young. Second, because the memory of how this came about is not even a pleasant one.'

She stared at him, mouth set in a tight line and again he wondered if he'd gone too far. Then she sighed, relaxed, slumping back in the chair and dragging the blanket more closely around her. 'Granddad,' she said. 'I need to tell you something but please, can you promise not to judge me for it?'

Clara was getting almost used to these late night visits, but, looking through the glass panel in the front door, was surprised to see that Ernst was not alone. The girl standing beside him had about her an aura of nervous excitement, something pent up that was about to be released.

'This is Jennifer,' Ernst told Clara when she opened the door. 'I know it's late, but may we come in?'

Clara stepped back, aware that the girl was staring at her with unnerving intensity.

'Jennifer has something to say to you.'

Clara closed the door wondering if this presaged a tirade of hate or something else. Something else, she decided. Ernst was not one to allow such cruel confrontation; not now.

It was clear that Jennifer could not wait. The secret she had carried, now outed once this evening could not remain concealed.

'I knew Rob,' she blurted suddenly. 'Mrs Beresford, Rob thought that my dad might be his.'

Eighteen

Jennifer sat on the floor of Clara's living room, legs crossed and her shoes off. She wore odd socks, Clara noted. Both stripy, but one red and green, one in shades of blue. Before her, spread out on the hearthrug, lay scattered photographs and stacked albums. She held one image in her hand, stared hard at it and then turned it over and handed it to Clara.

'Oh,' Clara gasped. Finally, she understood what her son had seen and the conclusions he had reached. She turned the image back over and examined the picture, wondering at the number of times she had looked at it and not grasped its possible significance.

'He showed you this?'

Jennifer nodded.

Ernst held out his hand. 'May I?'

Clara handed him the picture.

'Ah,' he said. 'But this is Denny.'

'Aiden,' Clara corrected softly. 'Aiden Ryan. If you'd said his name, I might have realized.'

'There was never a reason to. And I have never called him Aiden, he has always been Denny.'

'I know, I know. Everyone focussed on Hensel. No one said anything about Aiden Ryan or any connection that would have made sense of it. But I don't understand, how did this picture lead Rob to you? I've pictures of all sorts of people in here, why pick on this one?'

Jennifer took the picture back and examined it again. The face of her father, not much older than she was now, stared back at her. He looked different now, of course. Years had added weight and lines and greying hair, but he was still perfectly recognizable. As was the girl standing beside him.

96

Clara, grinning happily, her hand in Aiden's. Friends around them, mugging for the camera.

'We were celebrating the end of exams,' Clara said. 'Aiden grabbed my hand and pulled me into the middle of the group. It was such a good day. We were so relieved to get the tests over and done with I don't think we even cared if we'd passed or not.'

'You wrote the names on the back,' Jenny said. 'Look, everyone named and Rob . . . Rob knew some of the people. You still kept in touch with a couple of them. He said he found out where they lived by looking in your address book and told them he was trying to get a surprise party together. That he wanted to get as many people together as he could from your school days.'

Clara shuddered. 'What a horrible thought. And they swallowed that?'

'Apparently one gave him the brush off, and told him she thought it was a daft idea. The other, I think Rob said he was called Bill, he told Rob where a couple of the others lived and even gave him other names.'

'Hum, that sounds like Bill Price,' Clara said. 'He was always a bloody pain. And the heart drawn round Aiden's name, I suppose that gave it away, didn't it? God, that boy of mine knew how to put two and two together and make five, didn't he?'

'He said, if you'd actually told him anything, he wouldn't have had to do it. But he wanted to know. Wanted it so badly.'

'I'm beginning to see that. God, if I'd realized how much . . . He pestered a bit when he was younger but I always told him they weren't worth knowing. I told him, when he was eighteen, I'd tell him all he wanted to know and it would be up to him. Why the hell couldn't he have waited? He only had a few months to go. '

'Why was it so important that he didn't find out sooner?' Ernst enquired.

'Because . . . For God's sake, I didn't even tell my parents who Rob's father was. I didn't let on to my sister, though she probably guessed. Most people thought it must have been my boyfriend . . .'

'Aiden wasn't your boyfriend?'

'No.' Clara shook her head. 'Aiden was . . . I fancied him something rotten and he knew it. All the girls did, but he wasn't interested in anything . . . I mean . . .' She felt embarrassed. It was this girl's father she was talking about.

'He was seventeen,' Jennifer said matter of factly. 'He liked sex.'

Clara stared at her.

Ernst humphed uncomfortably.

Clara nodded slowly. 'I guess neither of us was much wiser than that,' she admitted. 'Jamie, my boyfriend, he was possessive, didn't like me even looking at other people. So, one night when we had a major row . . . One thing led to another. Then Jamie found out and, well, the rest as they say . . .'

'But you must have liked my dad, you drew a heart round his name.'

Clara laughed, but it was laughter on the verge of tears. 'That's the most stupid thing,' she said. 'I didn't draw that. My friend did, she was winding me up and threatening to show the picture to Jamie. He'd have gone mad if he saw me holding hands with Aiden. He heard about it, of course, and that didn't help, but, you know, things blew over and we made up. Then things happened with Aiden and . . . after that it was just me and Rob.'

Jennifer had been watching her intently. 'He didn't want to hurt you,' she said finally. 'He told me, you'd been on your own, bringing him up and no one gave a shit for either of you. He understood why you didn't want his dad back in your life but, I don't know, I think part of it was he thought my dad, his dad, owed you something. You'd struggled with money and no one had ever given you a hand. It hurt him, Clara. That was part of the reason. The other part was he just wanted to know about himself, you know, the part of him that you hadn't given him. He said he had all these feelings and thoughts buzzing round in his head and they weren't like anything you ever seemed to have. He'd get angry, flare up, and you were always so calm.'

Clara laughed harshly. 'Calm! Me, Lord no. I just learnt to hide my feelings, I suppose. He might have thought I was floating but I was paddling like mad just to keep from drowning. I wanted to protect him from all that. Surely, it's what a parent should do? Protect?'

Jenny shrugged. 'Sometimes it helps to know your mum and dad aren't perfect.'

They fell silent, considering her words, then Clara asked, 'But how did you meet Rob? How did he find you?'

She shrugged, as though it was obvious. 'He worked his way through the phone book,' she said. 'Then he came to have a look at us. My dad and one other bloke were the right age, but when he saw my dad he knew he was the one in the photograph.' Jennifer paused and bit her lip. 'This wasn't the first time,' she said. 'He'd been looking since he was fourteen or fifteen years old.'

'What?'

'He said he'd . . . investigated about seven different people but this time he thought he'd got it right.'

'Investigated? Who? I mean, what did he do?'

She shrugged. 'I don't know, exactly, but he'd start by finding out how long you knew people and if you'd known them a long time . . . he'd investigate.' She bit her lip again. 'I think he got a bit obsessed,' she added.

'Obsessed! How did I not notice? How could he do all this and I not know?'

Jennifer sighed. She was looking at Clara as though considering whether or not she should reply at all and if she did how far she should go. 'Rob did OK at school, didn't he?'

'Well, yes.'

'He had friends you liked and brought them home, or at least talked about them a bit.'

'Yes, and?'

'This last year he got drunk sometimes, but not so drunk he was falling over so you thought that was normal and OK. You were pretty sure he wasn't doing drugs. He liked girls and all the stuff you'd expect someone male and seventeen to like.' Jennifer shrugged.

99

'So,' Clara felt her anger rising. 'You're saying I didn't look any further than the obvious. You're telling me I didn't care about my son. You're saying . . .'

'No, none of that,' Jennifer said. 'Look, he didn't give you any reason to look for other stuff. He was doing the things you wanted him to do and he was getting on well with you. Rob thought you were pretty cool, actually. He was grateful, glad you got along. Like I said, he didn't want to hurt you, he just thought you were owed and it was the one thing he didn't agree on, that you should keep the truth about his dad from him. It isn't your fault he hid stuff. Everybody does.'

'No.' Clara was shocked, emphatic. 'I was never dishonest with Rob, with anyone.'

'You didn't tell your parents about my dad,' Jennifer pointed out. 'Look, Mrs Beresford, I don't want to hurt you. I liked Rob and I can't get my head around what he did to Uncle Adam. It just doesn't make any sense. I wanted to say something before, but can you imagine what it would be like to say to your dad, here, look, you've got a son you don't know about and we've been seeing one another. I mean, not in *that* way, just like friends. Rob wanted me to try and talk to him, to set up some kind of meeting, but I was scared and I didn't know how and then, all of a sudden, it was too late. It was all too fucking late.'

Clara was shocked, Jennifer swearing seemed oddly out of place. Most kids did it for affect, but this was born of genuine feeling and therefore had an effect.

'None of this gets us closer to understanding why,' Ernst said softly.

Jennifer rubbed her eyes and Clara saw that she was crying. 'I told Uncle Adam,' she said at last. 'Granddad, I wanted to talk to you, but there never seemed to be a time. Then Uncle Adam came for Mum's birthday and, he'd had a drink or two and I'd been allowed some wine and we sat on the stairs and talked like we always do . . . did . . . and then. After that. It all went wrong.'

'Beth's birthday,' Ernst mused. 'So, about a month before . . . he died. Did he tell you what he planned to do about it?'

Jennifer shook her head. 'I thought he must have forgotten, not taken me seriously. I don't know.'

Clara was exhausted. Another piece of the puzzle had fallen into place but there was so much else she wanted to know. How, for instance, had Rob made contact with this young woman, convinced her he was genuine and she should help. Right at this moment, though, she didn't feel she had the strength to pursue the matter further.

'So we still don't know what happened that night,' Ernst said. 'But at least we begin to see a connection between things.'

Clara shook her head. 'An imagined connection,' she said quietly. 'Jennifer, it's my fault, isn't it? This whole mess. My fault for not being open or honest. For him not being able to come to me.'

'He didn't think so,' Jennifer said, but she didn't sound convinced.

'Imagined?' Ernst asked. 'You said an *imagined* connection.'

'The trouble is,' Clara said softly. 'I was probably pregnant even before I slept with Aiden. He wasn't Rob's dad.'

Nineteen

It took some organizing, but the obvious thing, Clara had decided was to pool resources. It seemed to her – and to Ernst – that the problem of the police investigation; why it had revealed so few leads was down to two factors. The first was simply that they had stopped looking. The second, that they actually had no clue as to what questions to ask. It had been established by the post mortem that Rob had been drinking and taking some cocktail of methamphetamine and cannabis. The inference was, some chance encounter with the unfortunate Adam Hensel had led Rob to stab him. No one suggested that this was in character. The official report spoke of a tragic incident and hinted that this was just another indicator of the drug problem spreading into an erstwhile clean town. Clara almost laughed aloud at that inference; drugs had been part of the scene when she was Rob's age and probably long before. She wondered if the official report reflected official naiveté or genuine stupidity.

No one had connected Adam Hensel with Rob Beresford because, on the face of it, there would be no connection and, even had the police interviewed Jennifer, which, under the known circumstances they had no reason to do, she would probably not have confessed to knowing him. Clara could imagine that revelation adding to the girl's existing troubles. Why should she have made life harder for herself?

But now, Clara felt, the time for secrecy and half truth and even the sparing of feelings was long gone. She phoned Alec Friedman and told him her news, then demanded a meeting with him. Having got agreement on that, she saw to it that Ernst and Jennifer and Rob's friends were also appraised of her demands.

And, she thought, demand or command it had been. A new energy had flooded her mind, brought a restlessness to her body since Jennifer's visit and Clara could not keep still.

Alec arrived first, then Ernst, accompanied by Jennifer. Patrick, Charlie and a reluctant Becky kept the others waiting only for a few minutes before they too settled, perched on chairs or on cushions on the floor. Clara had brought tea and coffee pots on trays with mugs and milk. She set the sugar bowl down upon the low table and seated herself in the vacant chair.

'Now,' she said, nodding at Alec. 'No more secrets, no more lies. Everything there is to know, we share now. And we'll begin with you.'

Alec took two files from his briefcase – a present from Naomi he was still getting used to using; his usual style was a plastic carrier from the local supermarket. He glanced uncertainly at Clara. Personally, he thought this was a crazy idea. The two girls were looking daggers at one another, Becky taking in Jennifer's swelling belly and her eyes darting questions at Clara.

'The post mortem report,' he said. 'If Rob had been driving, he'd have been three times over the limit. On top of that, there were the drugs . . .'

Clara shuddered. 'I don't believe that,' she said. 'Rob wasn't into . . .'

'The tox results don't lie, Clara. I'm sorry.'

'Rob . . . did smoke stuff,' Becky said reluctantly, 'and did other stuff too. I don't know exactly what.'

'Becky, we said no lies. If you know something more . . . '

'I don't, Clara,' Becky told her indignantly. She jerked her chin towards Jennifer. 'Maybe you should ask *her*.'

'Why should I know? You were his girlfriend. *Supposedly*.'

'What do you mean, supposedly?'

'Girls, please!' Ernst frowned them both into silence. 'This is not the time or the place. Nor is it necessary.' He turned to Becky. 'My dear, Jennifer was no threat to you.'

Becky scowled but lapsed into silence.

Alec continued. 'We know that Rob left Charlie's party just after ten. By eleven fifteen, Adam Hensel was dead.

103

Now, we have no evidence that Rob got a taxi or caught a bus. In fact, there were no direct buses anyway. So, if he walked, which seems most likely, he could not have met up with Adam much before eleven o'clock. The confrontation, whatever presaged it, must have lasted for a very short space. We know that Adam was stabbed with his own knife, which begs the question, how did it come to be in Rob's hand?

'We know now, that Adam and Rob were not unknown to one another. Did they arrange a meeting? Did Rob contrive his argument with Becky so that he could keep that appointment? If that's so, it might explain why Adam was so far from home. The location does now make sense though, being only a few streets from where Jennifer, Adam's niece, and her family live.'

'Adam was visiting on that night,' Ernst confirmed. 'Beth said he called and asked if they'd be in. He didn't say why. She was glad to see him.'

'She thought it was odd, though,' Jennifer supplied. 'Uncle Adam wasn't exactly spontaneous.'

'No, no, he wasn't.'

'Which fact mitigates in favour of a prearranged meeting,' Alec noted.

'But, how did he know Adam Hensel?' Becky wanted to know.

'It wasn't really Adam that was the link,' Clara told her. 'It was Jennifer.'

'I knew it,'

'No, you don't know it,' Clara told her. 'Rob was looking for his father, you told me that. He thought the man he was looking for was Aiden Ryan. Jennifer is his daughter.'

Slowly, hesitantly, she explained what Rob had been about.

Alec left about a half hour later. There was little he could add. He felt guilty that he could promise no resources to look into these developments. He would tell his bosses, but he knew the case would be left on the back burner unless and until something more dramatic came to light. Nothing had changed as regard the outcome of the investigation. Rob was still guilty; Adam Hensel was still dead. Case solved.

He offered Patrick a lift home, was unsurprised when it was declined. Feeling oddly sorry for himself – after all, he'd joined the police force to solve problems, not be beaten by them – he made his way to Naomi's.

Naomi greeted him with her usual enthusiasm, though, he reminded himself, determined to wallow, she still hadn't allowed him to set a date for the wedding.

Napoleon nuzzled at his pockets, tail beating at Alec's leg. 'Sorry, old man, I don't have anything for you.'

'Makes a change,' Naomi observed.

'I've not eaten since breakfast,' Alec confessed. 'Been one of those days.'

She laughed. 'I cooked, yours just needs reheating. I figured you'd be round sometime tonight.'

'You are an angel.'

'No, just an ex cop used to missing meals. Well, did you have your meeting?'

'Yes, oh boy yes.'

'That good?'

'That good.'

He filled in the blanks while the microwave did its thing.

'Anything you didn't tell the family?'

He reached for a tray and carried food and a glass of beer through to the living room, flopped down on the sofa with it on his lap.

'Can't get anything past you, can I? No.' He cut into the pie. The crust had gone slightly soggy, but he was too hungry to care. 'Chicken, that's nice. No, it was just a rumour really, not even that, I suppose. Some woman phoned a few days after Adam Hensel was killed, she said he frequented prostitutes in Pinsent.'

'You follow it up?'

'Sure. No joy. We showed his picture to all the regular girls, trawled the streets, no joy at all. So, seeing as she'd insisted on being Mrs Anonymous, we listed it as a possible malicious call. Every high profile investigation gets its crank calls, you know that.'

'Yes and I know you're feeding that dog chicken.'

'I am not.'

'Alec. I could hear you blowing on it to cool it down and now I can hear him slobbering. No more.'

Alec shrugged apologetically at the dog. 'Sorry, old man, she's found us out again.'

'You corrupt that dog.'

'Corrupt? Never.'

'So, no dirt on Adam Hensel then?'

'Not that we found, but to be truthful, we didn't dig that hard. Open and shut case and the perp killed himself. After which, resources were diverted elsewhere.'

'Hmm . . .' Naomi was thoughtful. 'But what does your instinct tell you?'

'My instinct tells me that Hensel set up the meeting. I figure he wanted to warn Rob off. Things got nasty. My guess is that Hensel pulled the knife, seeing as it was his that seems a logical assumption. Rob either took it off him or they struggled and we'll probably never know which. Hensel winds up on the wrong end of the blade. End of story.'

'Not a very satisfactory end.'

'Is there ever a satisfactory end to something like this? No, Clara and Ernst Hensel will run it ragged for a while but they'll soon realize they can't achieve any more than we already have. There must have been a fight; a man ended up dead.'

'Was Hensel sober?'

Alec chewed and swallowed before replying. 'No. He was not. He'd been over at his sister's, left the car there saying he'd take a taxi. He had, according to the sister, had two, three glasses of wine. Her husband, Aiden, he reckons he put away more than that.'

'Dutch courage?'

'On both sides, probably. Booze, sharp pointy objects, lethal combination. Happens weekly on a street near you. The ironic thing is, Aiden was probably nothing to do with Rob. My money's on the boyfriend and Clara's still not putting a name to the sperm.'

'I'm going to have to tell the rest of the family about this meeting,' Ernst said regretfully.

'Do you have to, Granddad?'

'You can't keep going behind their back,' Clara said quietly. 'They'll be hurt even more; it's bound to come out sooner or later.'

'I suppose.' Jennifer shifted restlessly and stretched her legs out in front of her. She massaged the calf muscle; it was threatening to cramp. Again.

'When is the baby due?'

Jennifer looked up in surprise. The boy they'd called Patrick had barely spoken all evening and now he did it seemed an odd question for a boy to ask. 'Um, April. The fourth.'

He nodded. 'That must seem kind of scary. I'd be terrified.'

Jen blinked, surprised again. 'I am a bit.' She became aware that they were the focus of attention and blushed, looked away.

'We should go,' Charlie said. 'Clara, I'll call you. Let us know what you want us to do, OK?'

'Thanks, Charlie, but I think it's up to me now.'

He looked about to argue, then nodded sharply. 'We've got mock exams all week,' he said. 'I guess I should concentrate for a bit.'

'You should. Don't worry. I'm fine and I'll let you know if we find out anything more.'

'Well, goodbye then,' Becky said, just about including Jennifer in her farewell, though it was clear she still wasn't sure that this other girl was not a rival for Rob's affection after all.

Patrick hung back. He had scribbled something on a scrap of paper and he handed it to Jen. 'Um, my email,' he said. 'If you need someone to talk to. I mean . . .' He blushed scarlet and made a big thing of saying goodbye to Clara.

Ernst cast an amused look at Jennifer. 'Looks like you've made a conquest,' he said.

'Oh Granddad, don't,' Jennifer told him, but she slipped the scrap of paper in her pocket, oddly gratified.

Twenty

January the sixth was bitterly cold. Naomi could taste snow in the air. If it fell, and didn't just bugger off inland as every threat had done so far, it would be the first of the year. Naomi still possessed a childlike love of snow and ice, though these days, not being able to see the surface she walked on made her more wary. She had learned to trust Napoleon in most ways, but his four feet were more secure on any surface than were hers and this was still a major anxiety for her.

Today though, she hoped the snow would hold off for different reasons. She had persuaded Harry to drive her to Pinsent, to meet a contact from her police days. In her bag she had a picture of Adam Hensel, clipped from the local paper and then photocopied and enlarged. Harry reckoned it was still a clear likeness and, without pestering Alec for prints the investigation might have had access to, it was the best she could manage.

She hadn't yet told Alec of her plans and she hadn't yet told Harry that her informant was a prostitute. Harry could, on occasion, shock easily. Much more to the point, he also hated driving in snow, hence her worry about the threatened weather.

'It's looking a bit murky,' he told her halfway through their journey.

'We won't be long, I promise. We'll be back before dark and the forecast says it should hold off until then.'

'Tell that to those clouds. They're full of it. Must weigh a ton.'

'How's Patrick?' she asked to take his mind off things.

'Oh, all right, I suppose. Been spending a lot of time on

that chat thing these past few days. He's not looking forward to Monday.'

'Oh, are they back at college then?'

'Yes, so I expect he'll be reinstating his afternoon visits. You sure you don't mind? You've been very good about it.'

'I don't mind. He's welcome and he's got a key if I'm not there.'

'I know. I think that's very decent of you. He's no right to expect that much. Why are we going to Pinsent, anyway?'

'You could say I'm following a lead.'

'Oh, something to do with the Hensel thing?'

'Maybe. I can't be sure. I'm just chasing rumours.'

'And Alec doesn't know.'

She sensed he was rather glad to have been taken into her confidence when Alec had not. 'Alec doesn't know. It may be nothing after all.'

'Hmm. Right. Oh damn and blast.'

'What?'

'Snow,' Harry told her disgustedly. 'The forecast got it wrong again. I could do better with bloody seaweed.'

It was snowing more heavily by the time they reached Pinsent nine miles up the coast. This time of year there were spaces on the promenade and Harry parked, posting enough coins into the meter for a couple of hours. He helped Naomi out of the car and she was glad not to have brought the dog along. She shivered, pulling her coat and scarf more tightly and wishing she had thought to bring a hat.

'How far is it?'

'Along the promenade, to the right. It's about a four, five minute walk. A place called the Italian Club.'

'Sounds posh.'

'Delusions of . . . well of anything really. It's a little café, caters for the tourists that don't want chips. The last time I was there . . .' The last time she was there she had been able to see. 'Last time I was there it had those gingham curtains that come just halfway up the window.'

'And the woman we've come to see?'

'Um, last time I saw her she had a lot of dyed blonde hair. All piled up like a sixties beehive. I've never seen her wear

109

it any other way. In fact, I think it's been like that since it was actually in fashion. I doubt she's changed.'

'Sounds charming,' Harry mused. 'You know, you're going to catch your death, no hat.'

'I forgot. We must be nearly there. Can you see it?'

'Yes, actually, it's got a board outside. Is the food any good, I'm starving.'

'It's not bad. Least I can do is buy you lunch.'

Jodie was waiting for them inside. 'Ooh, look at you. You look great, love.'

'I probably look like a drowned rat.' Naomi shook her hair free of snow.

'And who's your friend?'

'This is Harry Jones. Harry, meet Jodie. Jodie, Harry. Oh, it's a bit warmer in here.'

'Harry, is it? I thought you were with that copper.'

'I am. Harry's a friend, a good friend. We've known one another for a long time.'

'Well, happy to meet you, love. Now, what was it you wanted?'

They sat down and ordered coffee. Naomi rummaged in her bag and found the photograph. 'You know him?'

She heard Jodie crinkle the paper and lay it flat on the table. 'Him,' Jodie said. 'That bloke that got himself killed. We've already had the locals asking about him.'

'Did you recognize him, Jodie?'

'God, love, you know I'm up front about what I do. Like I told them, I don't know him, don't know that any of the girls recognized him either.'

'No, I believe not, but I know you can ask in places we can't. It's important, Jo. Can you do me a favour and pass these out, get back to me if there's any gossip.'

'Surely. I can ask. I can't promise anything, though. Now, you tell me about yourself and how you're doing.'

'Is she um . . .'

'A professional lady? Yes. She's a dancer, or she was, then she got into management in a manner of speaking.'

'You mean she . . .'

110

'I mean she sets up dates with escorts. All very high class, runs her business out of a dress shop on Broad Street and, what I've heard, knows how to charge. Her girl's make a good living.'

'You condone it?'

'I like Jodie, she plays it straight. Someone works for her they see the money they earn. Jodie takes commission, she doesn't take the lot.'

'I still don't think it's right,' Harry protested. He shivered. 'It's snowing even harder. I'm not looking forward to the drive back. Does Alec know about her?'

'I expect Alec's arrested her as many times as I have,' Naomi said. 'She was on our patch before she moved up to Pinsent.'

'Oh, I see.'

'No, you don't, Harry,' Naomi laughed. 'No reason why you should.'

'Oh, but I want to.' He held the door open and helped her into the car before running around to the other side. 'I want to understand. You know, I've led a very sheltered life, I think.'

'You have a teenage son and you still manage to say that? Harry you amaze me.'

Harry chuckled then he said more seriously, 'What does this have to do with the Adam Hensel business?'

'Mmm, maybe nothing. Alec told me that after the murder a woman phoned in and said he used prostitutes in Pinsent. The intelligence was followed up, but nothing came of it. It could have been just a malicious call, of course.'

'People do that?'

'Oh, happens all the time. Some people feel this over-whelming need to be involved, so they call in with false information or, sometimes, it's genuine information but nothing to do with the case.'

'I've heard that people confess. To things they didn't do, that is.'

'It happens.'

'And you think this was more than a malicious call?'

'Let's say, I'm curious.'

111

'You know what curiosity did.'

'So I'm told. The thing is, you see, Alec's hands are tied. So far as his Superintendent is concerned, the case is well, not closed exactly, but as good as. It's solved, in as far as they're pretty certain Rob did the deed. Poking around at the edges isn't going to bring either Rob or Adam Hensel back.'

'So, you thought you'd do your bit.'

'So I thought I'd use what investigative talent I still have . . .'

'What considerable talent you have.'

'Thank you. What considerable talent I have, to do my own poking around the edges. Besides, I know as well as you do what not knowing can do. It eats you up inside and from what I've seen of Clara she deserves better than that. So, for that matter do Patrick and his friends.'

Harry nodded. 'I'll second that,' he said with feeling. 'Naomi, if there's anything I can do. You only have to let me know.'

Twenty-One

Ernst stood in the hallway of his son's flat not wanting to go further inside and yet knowing that he must. No one had wanted to enter the flat since he died, but the pressure was now on to put it on the market and get rid. Ernst wanted to look around before his daughter and son-in-law came in to clear the place of any personal effects. There was talk about bringing in one of the local house clearance firms to do the job; no one wanted to empty Adam's flat. To do so was the final acknowledgement that he would not be coming back.

He didn't know what he was looking for or if he'd recognize that significant something should he see it, but Ernst felt he had to try. Alec's suggestion that Adam may have set up the meeting that led to his death was one that made sense. Maybe Ernst would have reached that conclusion on his own, in time, but it had shocked him to be confronted by it. Shocked him more to realize how reasonable an assumption it was.

What had happened after Jennifer had told Adam about Rob? Had he spoken to the boy? Had he tried to find out about him? And why drink so much before the meeting? Was it Dutch courage or was it simply that he didn't see Rob as a threat?

Ernst figured that if the evidence for any of this existed, it would be in the flat. Adam's personal effects had been returned to him and Ernst had gone though them again today but there was nothing exceptional. Adam's wallet, with cards and money, his mobile phone – the numbers were all ones Ernst expected to be there – a few coins, his keys, a shopping list and a couple of till receipts. Normal things. Unremarkable items.

The hall was tidy and empty but for a small table; a

113

Victorian plant stand, actually, Ernst noted, on which Adam sat the phone. The shelf beneath held directories and a small green book in which he had written telephone numbers. Again, only family, friends, work colleagues. Adam had been meticulous enough to state which was which. He had always been organized, finicky even, Ernst thought. Even as a little boy his toy shelves had been organized according to type of toy, or colour, or shape, whatever his present mood might be. Elizabeth piled her possessions into a big chest and could never find anything. It was a common theme of childhood arguments that Elizabeth couldn't find her pencils and wanted to borrow his. Or that she left their paints with the colours all muddied. Or that his books came back with the corners turned down when she borrowed them. In the end, Ernst had told Beth that she must use only her own things and that if she didn't leave Adam's toys alone, he would give him a padlock for his door to keep her out. He never did and Elizabeth never really ceased to annoy her brother with her messy ways. They simply grew up and their interests differed and Adam's possessions held less appeal.

Ernst left the hall and wandered through the first door into the living room. Here there was the impression that Adam had just stepped out for a moment and would soon be home. A newspaper lay on the coffee table, folded and placed square with the corner. The tidiness of the room marred only by the soft fall of dust which now covered every surface, something Adam would not have permitted.

Ernst opened the sideboard drawers, the cupboards, rifled quickly and carefully through the bills and letters, the stacked plates and china cups. He recognized the remnants of a dinner service he and Lisle had bought not long after their marriage. He hadn't even noticed it was missing, and that Adam had it safe both irritated and yet pleased him. Adam's computer stood on an oak table Ernst had given him. It had come from the family home and, when he'd moved to a smaller place after Lisle's death, Adam had asked if he could have this and a few other pieces for the flat.

It took Ernst a moment or so to find the on button, finally discovering it on the back of the tower unit and not at all where he expected it to be. Typical, somehow, for Adam to be different and just a little difficult. He waited for it to fire up, thinking how like this process was to turning on his old valve radio. He could go and make a cup of tea while it did its thing. He recalled Adam saying that this was an old machine and he should think about updating it, but, as he only used it for the odd letter and to do his accounts, anything more sophisticated seemed a waste. Ernst sat down and clicked the mouse on 'My Documents'. Somewhat to his surprise, a blue screen appeared with instructions to input the password.

'Password?' Ernst was taken aback. 'What on earth did he have to protect with a password?'

He closed the window and tried 'my computer' got the same response. The blue screen again with the password prompt.

Ernst stared at the offending screen, puzzled and irritated. What password would his son use? How many chances would he get? He had a vague memory of Jennifer saying that you got three tries before the machine locked up. She'd been criticizing a television programme they were watching, hadn't she?

Reluctantly Ernst closed the whole thing down wondering who he could ask about password protection. Would Jennifer know what to do? Ernst wasn't sure anyway that he should involve her.

Feeling like an intruder he searched the kitchen and bedroom. There were papers and letters in the bedside cabinet on the right hand side of the bed but nothing that related obviously to his quest. The left hand cabinet was empty.

Would he even know if something was out of place? Would he be aware of it if he found something relating to Rob?'

Ernst honestly didn't know. He glanced again at the empty cabinet. Suzanna, he thought, his son's ex-wife. It was really nothing to do with her any more but she had lived here and she might, just might be able to see what he could not. She had obviously still cared enough to have come to the funeral. Should he ask her to help him now?

115

He couldn't recall her number but, hadn't he seen it in the green book. Ernst hurried though to the hall. Yes, it was there and, to his amusement, Adam had written next to it the abbreviation 'ex' as though he might be able to forget just who she was. The amusement was tempered with regret. His son had always been a bit of an odd ball, he thought, but for all that – or perhaps because of it – Ernst loved him deeply and missed him so much it hurt. It hurt more when he thought of the last time they had met, a few days before Adam died. They hadn't argued or even been in conflict, but they hadn't really talked either. They had, instead, exchanged just the surface information about their respective lives. The how are you, fine thank you sort of interchange that might have passed between acquaintances and not close kin.

Twenty-Two

E rnst arrived at his daughter's house and walked into the middle of a row. It didn't take a genius to work out that Jennifer had told them about Rob. Her timing, Ernst thought, left something to be desired. He'd told her he would tackle the subject with Beth sometime over the next few days, but that he would do so gently. He could well imagine that Jennifer, having practised by revealing her secret to him and then elaborated on the disclosure at the meeting with Clara and the others, would most likely have blurted the whole thing without preliminaries. Or, worse still, in revenge or response to some disagreement with her mother.

Aiden opened the front door when Ernst rang the bell – the volume of the dispute, if not the words, had been audible in the drive-way. He took one look at Ernst and then gestured at the room beyond from which the sound of furious female voices issued.

'You sort it,' he said. 'I've said my piece, now I'm off down the pub.'

He grabbed his coat from the peg and strode off into the dusk. Ernst wondered if he could join him without the women of the house noticing, but that seemed cowardly, particularly as he, it could be said, had conspired with his granddaughter in some respects.

Instead, he closed the front door, took a deep breath and crossed the expanse of Victorian tiled hall.

The evidence of Beth's rage seemed to extend to the very roots of her short blonde hair. She crackled with fury, face flushed, eyes blazing with it. The static charge of her anger lifting the tresses from her head and the fibres of her mohair sweater.

117

Jennifer, no less incensed, faced her mother and screamed across the six inches of distance between them. At first, so concentrated was the sound of pure rage that Ernst failed to make out the words, then, as he focused, the battle lines began to coalesce

'I've done nothing wrong!' Jennifer screeched.

'Nothing! Colluded. Deceived. You're no daughter of mine. Get out of my house. Just get out of my sight.'

So, it had gone that far. 'Beth, Beth,' Ernst cried. 'Be calm. This will do no good.'

She hadn't registered him until then, but both women turned now and Ernst felt himself physically lashed by the wave of bitterness. Beth's because he had kept her in the dark. Jennifer's, less forceful – she'd not had her mother's experience – but generated by her resentment that he had not been there when she had to face her mother with this truth. The fact that she and not Ernst had picked the instant of revelation an irrelevance.

'You! Just what the hell did you think you were doing? Jen I can almost forgive. She's a child, but you!'

'Beth, calm down. No one has done anything . . .'

'Not done anything? She *knew* Adam's killer and she didn't say a bloody word. Not a bloody word and then you, instead of telling me about her little liaison, you go behind my back and see that woman. That woman. For all I know, *he* could be the father of the little bastard she's carrying. Now wouldn't that be just perfect.'

'Beth. Enough.'

She stopped in her tracks and drew herself up and in, her father's command cutting through the weight of years. It might have calmed then, but Jennifer was not so adept at recognizing the moment.

'You stupid bitch,' she yelled. 'I thought he was my bloody brother! Yeah, right, like I was going to fuck my brother.'

Beth wheeled around, hand raised and Ernst was almost tempted to let it find its target. He sighed, swore under his breath and then stepped between the warring factions.

'Enough! No more.'

Beth froze. She stared at her father and lowered her hand.

118

She was shaking and, Ernst saw, she had begun to cry. He wanted to take her in his arms and rock her as he had when she'd been a little girl. To hold her tightly while she cried. But he knew he couldn't. She'd resent that weakness almost more than she resented what he'd done. It would be to admit that he might not be as guilty as she painted him but the pain was too raw for her to let go of it just yet.

And then there was Jennifer, sniffing and snivelling and equally in need of love.

'Dad, just get her out of here. Please. I can't cope with this.'

The hurt in her voice cut him to the core but it told him also that this would pass, given space and time. He nodded. 'Jennifer,' he said without taking his eyes from his daughter's face, 'go and pack a bag. You can stay with me for a few days.'

'Damn right I will,' Jennifer exploded. 'And don't think I'm coming back.'

She fled the room leaving her elders alone. Beth held up a hand. 'Don't say anything, Dad, I couldn't bear it, OK?'

Ernst nodded. 'I'll go,' he said. 'But Bethy . . .'

'No, I said not a word. Please, Dad.'

He nodded again and left the room, went to sit on the stairs, Jennifer and Adam's favourite roost, while his daughter wept and his granddaughter slammed around upstairs packing her bags and vowing never to come back home.

Twenty-Three

Aiden's local was the Rose a couple of streets away. Ernst told Jennifer to stay in the car, the tone of his voice such that she didn't argue. He went inside, finding Aiden playing darts in the Lounge Bar.

Aiden glanced his way, played his shot before coming over, carrying his beer.

'What do you know about all this mess then?'

'I know that Rob, the boy who killed Adam, he thought you might be his father.'

'His father?'

'You knew his mother. Clara. Clara Beresford.'

'Clara . . . Rob Beresford. His name was Rob Beresford? The police said they knew who it was, that he committed suicide, they never told us his name. I . . . How did you find out?' He sat down in the nearest chair. 'You want a beer?'

'No, no, I have Jennifer in the car. She's coming to me for a few days.'

'Oh. Right. Clara.' Aiden was stunned. 'But how did you know? Did the police tell you?'

Ernst shook his head. 'I read the papers, watch the news. The police also told me that the killer took his own life. One even mentioned how, though I don't think he even noticed his slip. So, I went through the newspaper reports and I found the story. There was only one. A boy, who killed himself by jumping from a bridge into the canal. It did not give his name, but mentioned the district where he lived. I went there, drank in the local pubs, chatted to the landlord and the locals. Everyone knew who it was. Most felt grief for the mother and said how terrible it must be for her. I watched the papers for the funeral. I knew they would say something about such loss of a young life. There was no connection made to my son, but the boy, Robert, he was only seventeen and his name protected by the law which, concerning his mother, is as it should be. I followed her home after the funeral. Then, I went to visit her.'

'You went . . . why? For God's sake, what did you plan to do?'

Ernst shrugged. 'I no longer know, Denny, and it was only much later as small things emerged that we realized a connection was in fact there, between my son and Clara's. The connection was you.'

'But . . .' Aiden reached for his beer, but his hand was shaking. 'Was he mine? My God, was he mine?'

Ernst shook his head. 'Clara believes not,' he said. 'We may not ever know for certain.' He looked around at the early evening drinkers and the wooden tables, bright red walls. This was not the place for such intimate revelations, but it had to be told and, if he invited Aiden back to his home, Jennifer would be there to interrupt and interfere.

'You knew she was pregnant?' Ernst asked.

Aiden nodded. 'Yeah. I was shit scared she'd . . . she'd name me. We had sex once. That was it.'

'She didn't name you,' Ernst said. 'In fact, she was adamant that neither you nor the boyfriend who seemed the other choice should be involved. All those years, she managed on her own. Clara says you were something of a bad influence,' he said fondly. 'That you were not capable of being serious or being there for her and she felt you and the other one no longer had a place in her life.'

Aiden smiled, half sad, half, Ernst thought, flattered. 'I wasn't much of a catch then,' he admitted. He laughed. 'I cultivated the wild child image, fast bikes, running with the wrong crowd.'

Looking at the middle-aged man in his grey slacks and comfortable wooly sweater, Ernst found that touchingly hard to believe. 'We were all young once,' he said softly. 'Young and stupid.' He reflected sadly that some don't get past that age.

'I think our Jen is starting to realize that,' Aiden said. 'You

121

know, this makes me wonder . . .' He looked embarrassed. 'That it might be in the blood, you know. Me and Clara and Rob . . . if, if I was . . . you know. And Jen and whoever.' He paused, reached for his pint and managed to hold on this time, took a long swallow. 'She's not . . . told you who, has she?'

Ernst shook his head. They talked for a little longer, Ernst filling in what gaps Jennifer's explosive confrontation had left out and warning Aiden of what reception he was likely to receive at home. Then he went back to a now complaining Jennifer and drove her to his flat, settling her in before telling her he needed groceries if she planned to stay. Ernst himself ate simply and the cupboards weren't exactly stocked to teenage requirements.

He stocked up at the local supermarket, loading the trolley with a combination of what he termed 'real food' and the kind of junk he knew she liked. Impulse took him back to the Edwardian road where Adam had died.

Sitting in the cul de sac, opposite the road sign, he could see the flowers he had laid, faded now and brown behind their plastic wrapper. It pleased him that no one had tidied them away but he, always a tidy man, felt grieved too at the unsightliness.

What had happened here?

Ernst sat in the rapidly cooling car and closed his eyes, behind the lids he could visualize the scene. His son, waiting on the corner. The young man, Rob, crossing the road, standing just a little away from him, uncertain and maybe just a little scared. Adam wouldn't have been scared. He brimmed with confidence and oozed a quiet authority. Would the boy have felt threatened by that? Adam could appear arrogant. That could intimidate and aggravate. Lord knows, Ernst thought, it sometimes aggravated *him* and *he* loved his son.

He could see them now, easy to visualize, he had spent so long studying Rob's picture he fancied he could even see the gestures, the body language, the way he walked and moved. He saw Rob gesture, see the attitude – the Jennifer type attitude – in his gestures and the shrug of his shoulders. See as he threw his hands up in a gesture of dismissal as he half turned away. Could imagine Adam's response. Sarcastic, maybe. Assertive certainly.

The boy would have turned back then, aggressive, irritated at another adult who failed to see his point of view. The anger Clara talked about would have flared and . . .

Ernst opened his eyes unable to cope with the film that played out behind the closed lids.

He felt chilled. Stiff. Old. His eyes blurred and he blinked hard, then wiped them with gloved hands.

'Adam. What the hell was going on? That's all I want to know.'

All Rob wanted was to be taken seriously. To be told, as Jennifer had been certain this man would, that he would get a hearing. That maybe they could find out the truth once and for all. Rob had been saving for years now, knowing that a DNA test would sort things out once and for all. He tried to tell this man that was all he wanted but all he got back was scorn. Advice to go home and leave them all alone.

Alone, that's the way Rob had always been. Rob and Clara. Clara and Rob and a wall of silence and he was never expected to complain.

Twenty-Four

Jodie was as good as her word and called Naomi on the Monday afternoon.

Only one girl remembered Adam. Would Naomi like to set up a meeting with her?

'Yes,' Naomi told her. That would be great and yes, she could get to Jodie. If necessary, she'd take a taxi.

'Take a taxi where?' Patrick wanted to know. He was seated at her computer, trying to construct an essay on the life and work – and influence on Patrick's artwork – of David Hockney. So far as Naomi could tell, Hockney hadn't had any particular influence, but Patrick said his teacher didn't think Frank Miller or Neil Gaiman were suitable subjects for an AS level essay.

'To see a contact,' Naomi told him.

'A contact? What kind of contact? Someone you used to know?'

'Yes, someone I used to know.'

'Who? Is this anything to do with Dad taking you to Pinsent? He wouldn't tell me anything about it.'

'Not everything is your business,' Naomi laughed.

Patrick grimaced. 'Is this to do with Rob?'

'What makes you think that?'

'I know you,' he said pointedly. 'I can't see you leaving everything to Alec.'

Naomi laughed. 'It's just a rumour that didn't get followed up at the time,' she said. 'I thought of someone who might have some answers so I went to see her.'

'But you can't tell me about it.'

'If it comes to anything I will,' Naomi promised and Patrick, reluctantly, had to be satisfied.

124

Discussion was interrupted by Alec's arrival and he had something for Patrick to look at.

'I've talked to my boss,' he said. 'But you've got to understand this is still unofficial but . . . anyway, take a look, Patrick, see if you notice anything odd.'

'What is it?' Naomi asked. She heard the slide open on the CD drive and Patrick clicking the mouse.

'Copies of the files on Rob's computer,' Alec told her. 'Not all of his emails, unfortunately, they were password protected and I'm still waiting on forensics to get back to me on that. It's slipped down the priority list,' he added irritably. 'We've managed to get what was on the school system and they'd already pulled some of his chat room files off the hard drive. Nothing revealing that we could see . . .' He left the comment hanging.

'But *I* might, or Becky, or Charlie,' Patrick said. He sounded excited and Naomi frowned.

'Should you really be getting Patrick involved?' she asked.

'Probably not and we ought to check with your dad,' Alec conceded. 'I just feel bad about things. I tried to get some bodies allocated to this today, but no one can be spared apparently.' He sounded even more irritable, remembering, Naomi assumed, the bureaucratic minefield he must have been walking through all day.

'I'm just looking at stuff, Nomi,' Patrick assured her. 'What harm can it do?'

'Well, if Harry agrees, you can take that copy away, but I'll need it back. The official line is I've taken it to show to a computer expert. Thankfully no one asked me to specify what kind. Yet.'

'Cool,' Patrick was impressed by the fudged truth. 'So now I'm an expert.'

'So now you've got an essay on Hockney.' Naomi reminded him.

'It doesn't have to be in until Thursday.'

'By which time you'll have more homework. Come on, Patrick, get the bad stuff out of the way first, then you can play. You've got to check it out with Harry anyway.'

'I'm not five,' Patrick said, objecting to her tone, but he

125

was laughing too. 'OK, OK, I'll get the first draft done tonight. Deal?'

'Deal. And don't think just because I can't see what you're doing I can't tell the difference between composition and detection.'

'Naomi,' Patrick said grandly. 'Credit me with some sense. Like I'd try to fool you.'

'Hmm, I'm trying to decide if you're just being patronizing or trying for irony. Coffee?' she asked Alec.

'Thanks.'

He followed her through to the kitchen and leant against the counter while she ground beans and played with the filter. 'Dinner smells good.'

'I've just made a casserole. I thought we could do with something to keep out the chill. It's been a lousy day. I hate melting snow about as much as I love the dry stuff. I had a phone call,' she went on.

'From?'

'Jodie Stuart. Remember her?'

'Jodie the Madame. Of course I do and why would she be ringing you? Or do I really have to ask?'

'No, don't suppose you do. I got Harry to run me over to Pinsent on Saturday. I'd have told you about it sooner or later.'

'Oh, would you really.'

'Well, yes. I'm telling you now, aren't I? Anyway,' she went on allowing no room for his objections, 'I saw her and I asked about Adam Hensel.'

'I'm sure the local beat officers already spoke to Jodie and her girls.'

'Yes, well. Jodie owes *me*. Anyway, I've got a lead the locals didn't. Jodie's set up a meeting for tomorrow afternoon.'

'In Pinsent? How are you getting there? Not that you should be going at all.'

'Oh and why not?'

'Because . . . because it isn't your job any more.'

'Oh? And it's your job to recruit a seventeen-year-old "computer expert", is it?'

126

'That's different.'

'Is it? Alec, I'm not doing anything dangerous. Jodie and I go way back and if I can get an angle we haven't covered, surely it's worth a little trip up the coast.'

'I suppose,' Alec said reluctantly. 'She didn't tell you anything more? Just that this woman recognized Adam Hensel.'

'Not much, no. It sounds as though she worked for Jodie for a while, but she's on her own now. An escort, Jodie said. She described her as very classy.'

'Classy by Jodie's standards? Hmm, anything that isn't a complete dog.'

'Oh, bitchy. Anyway, I'm meeting her tomorrow and we'll see what we do see. That sounds like Harry,' she added as the door bell rang. 'I'll let you do the talking, shall I?'

Twenty-Five

Apart from the funeral, Ernst and Suzanna Hensel had met only twice since she had divorced his son. It wasn't that they had parted on bad terms; not even Adam had managed to do that, Suzanna being a genuinely pleasant soul. It was simply that the circumstances which had once brought them together had now drifted them apart and there had simply been no reason to fight the inevitable.

They still exchanged Christmas cards and, when Suzanna had remarried, both Ernst and Adam had sent their greetings, blessings and a little gift. Ernst knew that seemed strange, but the fact was, neither he nor Adam bore Suzanna any malice for the break-up of the marriage. Adam had made no concessions even when another person came to share his home and partake of his life. The amazement had been that Adam had managed to persuade anyone to marry him at all.

'What attracted you?' Ernst asked her.

'He made me laugh. He was intelligent, kind. He caught me on the rebound from "The Big Romance". I decided I was better off with intelligent and kind and safe. I was right, for a while.'

It was strange, Ernst thought, how easily he had slipped back into such intimate conversation. 'And you are happy now?'

'Oh yes. Clive is both intelligent and kind and "The Big Romance". It works better, you know, when the other partner in the marriage notices you exist.' Her smile softened what might have been harsh words. 'Adam didn't need or want a wife. He wanted an equal partner in a business arrangement. One that provided conversation and support and sex, but which could be timetabled and organized and dismissed when necessary. I thought I might be able to change him.' She laughed. 'Some hope of that.'

'And Clive. You hope to change him?'

'No,' she shook her head. 'One thing I learnt from Adam was that you should examine the goods thoroughly before making the purchase. Marriage is a case of "buyer beware". You shouldn't fool yourself into thinking that a person has certain qualities or attributes, just because you hope they will acquire them in time.'

Ernst thought of his own wife, his beloved Lisle. She surprised him constantly. Life long he never felt he truly knew every part of her. He missed her so much. Life had seemed a lot flatter, blander since she had gone.

'It seems so strange to be back here,' Suzanna said, observing the place that had once been her home too.

'It must be. I'm grateful for you coming here. Especially under the circumstances.'

She pursed her lips and nodded. 'It's a terrible thing, Ernst. An appalling thing.' She fell silent for a moment or two, turning slowly on the same spot and interrogating the neat, blandly furnished room. 'Now, she said. 'What is it we're looking for?'

For the next hour they examined paperwork and searched the room for clues. Moving into the bedroom and then the kitchen, Suzanna recalling that Adam kept utility bills in one of the kitchen drawers.

It was no surprise to Ernst, knowing the meticulous and habitual qualities his son possessed, that Suzanna should still know where all things were kept and that Adam still kept them there. She noticed some changes.

'He has a mobile phone now,' she said. 'The bills are here.' She looked surprised. 'He used it a lot too.'

'I remember Jennifer teaching him to text,' Ernst said.

'The computer looks the same, though. God, it came out of the ark. He got it a year or so before I left. Did he still use it?'

'I believe so. He said it wasn't worth upgrading. He wrote letters and did his accounts, that was all. But it's a funny thing, Suzanna, he protected it with a password. Why would he do that?'

'I don't know.' She frowned. 'Come to think of it, yes, I remember he did that. I had my laptop and never used his machine, but . . . You know, Ernst, I'd make a bet he hasn't changed it.'

'And do you know this password?'

'I did,' she said cautiously.

'Can you remember? Try, Suzanna. Please try.'

They fired up the antiquated machine and she pulled up a chair, sat frowning at the screen. 'It was something really stupid,' she said. 'Something really Adam.' She sat and thought some more until Ernst was persuaded that she could not recall – after all, why should she after all this time? Then she leaned forward, her fingers tapping away at the keys. She clicked the return key and the blue screen faded out, the familiar icons began to appear.

'You did it? Suzanna, you're a genius.'

'No, just have a memory for stupid things. There were two related words and for a little while I just couldn't think which.'

'And in the end.?'

'Oh. Compulsive. That was the password. I couldn't remember if it was that or Obsessive. I guessed right.'

'A very Adam thing,' Ernst agreed softly. 'Very Adam.'

Twenty-Six

In the end, Naomi had an escort to Pinsent for her meeting with Jodie; Alec decided that he could call it police business and so drive her there. She refused point blank to let him come with her into the café, making him go for a long walk along the promenade.

'Jodie might not be bothered, but we don't know about this other woman. I want her to talk to me, not do a runner out the back door. Go for a walk. The fresh air's bracing. I'll phone you when I'm done.'

Jodie called to her, 'Over here, love, let me give you a hand.'

Naomi felt around the entrance door with her cane, vaguely remembering there had been a small step. She felt someone take her arm. It was Jodie. 'Right this way. Sit yourself down. This is Angel, the young lady I was telling you about.'

Naomi took a seat and extended a hand. 'Pleased to meet you.'

'Hello. Right. Um, I'm Angel. Well, it's Angela really but Angel is better for the work. More appealing to the clientele.' She giggled nervously.

'Thanks for meeting me,' Naomi told her. 'Oh, a cappuccino, please.' She moved her hands cautiously across the table top, mapping out the objects already on the table before her drink arrived.

'Jo says you were . . .'

'A Detective Sergeant. Yes. Car accident,' she added, anticipating the next question.'

'Wow. How do you manage?'

'Very well, really. I have good friends and I have a dog, though he's not much use to me today. We're off his normal

131

route.' The 'wow', Naomi thought, made her sound very young. She wondered how old Angel was, what she looked like.

'Sorry? I thought they could take you anywhere you wanted to go.'

Naomi smiled. 'No, they have to be trained for familiar routes. Napoleon is intelligent, but he can't read maps yet.'

Angel giggled. 'Right. I never really thought about it. So, if you want to go to your local shop, or something . . .'

'Napoleon can help me get there. He knows all the places I visit regularly and we're adding stuff all the time, but it's been a bit of a learning curve. For both of us.' She was used to this kind of curiousity now. People asking questions with varying levels of shyness or discomfort. But always the curiosity. At first, she'd resented it terribly and given any interrogator, however benign, short shrift. Slowly, she had learnt that people were just trying to build bridges and that it could actually be a way of getting them to talk about themselves.

'I couldn't do it,' Angel informed her emphatically.

'I didn't think I could either, but life goes on and you have to shift your boundaries to match. I don't think I could do your job.'

'Oh, well, no.'

Naomi bit her lip. 'I mean, I don't have the looks for it anyway, or the figure.'

'Oh, I don't know. Change the hair a bit, and some men go for the skinnier birds anyway. My clients tend to prefer the voluptuous, you know.' Naomi felt the table shift slightly as she leant forward. 'Do you know how much these boobs cost? Mind you, he did a fantastic job and if you want the real money, you have to invest, same as anything. Speculate to accumulate as they say.'

Jodie set the coffee down in front of Naomi. 'Can you find it OK?' she said anxiously. 'Your friend the other day, I noticed he helped you.'

'Harry fusses over me,' Naomi said. 'I let him because he likes it and it's nice sometimes. But yes,' she felt carefully, finding the rim of the saucer and then the handle of the cup.

132

'Right you are,' Jodie said. 'You two been getting acquainted?'

'Like a house on fire,' Naomi said. 'How long have you been working?'

'Oh,' Angel thought. 'For myself, the past five years. It's been a good move. I advertise and I pay my taxes and I've got my own little flat that I never take the clients to.'

'No?'

'Nope, no way. I'm an escort, now. I employ a guy to take me where I need to go, pick me up when I'm done and check in with me every hour if it's a new client. First sign of trouble, he knows what to do. A bunch of us share the security costs, you know.'

Naomi nodded. Jodie had always used this system with her girls. It kept the pimps out of the equation. Privately, Naomi wished all sex workers could be as organized.

'So, as an escort, it's more than just sex?'

'Sure. Dinner, nice hotel, payment in advance. My security guy takes it for me, though for the regulars we can do Visa now and Debit.'

'Really? How does it appear on the statement?'

'Oh, I'm also a personal trainer and life coach,' Angel said without any trace of irony. 'I took the courses and got the certificates. Of course, I keep that side separate and my other clients don't know about the more intimate services.' She paused. 'I get a lot of women coming to me too. In fact, another year or two and I'll switch the whole of my business over to that side. Go completely legit.'

Naomi nodded. 'Impressive,' she said. 'And Adam Hensel. Which sort of client was he?' She sipped her coffee. It was still far too hot.

'The man in the picture you mean? He didn't call himself Adam or Hensel. He was Ian Manning for all the time I've known him, though, of course, there may have been a different name on the credit card, there often is. They seem to just hope we won't notice. And he was, well, a bit different.'

'Oh? How?'

'Oh,' Angel said matter of factly. 'We often had dinner and a chat. He liked to talk, and if he booked a room, it would be for the night, though I never stayed that long. An hour was usually plenty for what he wanted.'

'And what did he want?'

'Well, I'm telling you, that was the funny thing. Ian or Adam or whatever he was called, he'd just sit there while I did my thing. He was a voyeur, I suppose. He didn't *do* anything, in fact, I was never even sure he could, if you get what I mean; he just liked to watch.'

'Doesn't mean anything,' Alec said as they drove home. 'Being a voyeur doesn't equate with being impotent.'

'No, I know. Besides, Angel said he used her website as well. It's subscription only past the first couple of pages, and he paid with the same credit card. She only gives the web address out to specific customers, but—'

'You got it from her.'

'Sure did. I think she agreed to give it to me because she can't for the life of her see how I'd make use of it.'

'Hmm, shows a distinct lack of imagination on her part, I'd say.'

'Oh?'

'Sure, you can listen and I can do the descriptions.'

'Alec Friedman. You should be ashamed. Anyway, it's another piece of information. Worth checking his credit card statements, just to make sure, isn't it?'

'Well yes, but another piece of information leading to what? He's a single man, who is maybe taking the safe sex message more seriously than most. I don't know, Naomi, I'm reluctant to stir things up any more than I have to if that's all there is to it. The family have been through enough. Some people get terribly upset if they think their loved one has been paying for sex. However discreet they were about it.'

'Oh, I know. But I also think we've got to keep going on this one. Now we've opened the can of worms, it seems cowardly to slam the lid back on without . . . I don't know, doing whatever you do with worms in a can.'

'I know, I know. It just goes against the grain, digging the dirt when the poor bugger's already dead and nothing's going to change that. Surely, the family will be better off remembering him as they do now.'

134

'You think it's such a big thing? Him using an escort? He didn't even have sex with her.'

'What I think is neither here nor there. Anyway, it gets us no closer to knowing what Rob had against him.'

'True. But we should travel hopefully. No, don't roll your eyes.'

'You don't *know* I rolled my eyes.'

'Oh yes I do. Supersonic hearing I've got now. I can hear them scraping round the sockets. You always roll your eyes when I come out with platitudes.'

'Or clichés.'

'Or anything else you don't want to hear. No, I suggest we go home, log on and try out Angela's web site. You can do the description part, just like you said.'

Twenty-Seven

The day had dragged for Patrick and his friends, knowing that they had Rob's files to look at and hoping for some miraculous breakthrough. They had gone straight to Patrick's place after school, hoping to grab a couple of hours to get on with things, though both Charlie and Becks had mock exams this week and knew they couldn't spare much time. Revision, onerous as it was, had to be done.

They had been expecting . . . what? None of them was quite prepared to say, but the reality of it was disappointing. Rob seemed to have kept his schoolwork on the machine from the year dot.

'I remember doing that essay,' Becky said. 'I think we were in year eight. What's he doing keeping that?'

They tried to be methodical, opening files and skimming them, but most proved as boring as the essay questions had been when they were first set, and the emails that Alec had managed to obtain were of the 'When's the math's homework due in?' or 'I've lost my question sheet, can you scan yours and send it otherwise I'm in deep shit' type.

'He really should have a clear out every now and again,' Charlie said. 'How can anyone keep so much dross?'

Patrick didn't like to point out that Charlie had used the present tense.

In the middle of all this, his machine chimed happily and a box popped up saying that one of his MSN contacts had signed it.

Patrick saw who it was and hesitated. His machine was set to sign him in automatically and he'd forgotten about Jennifer.

'Um, I'll just tell her I can't talk,' he said and opened a

window. Jen was saying hi, sending smileys with googly eyes.

'Who's that?' Becky wanted to know. She frowned. 'You're talking to that bitch from the other night?'

'She isn't a bitch,' Patrick objected. 'Becks, you don't even know her.'

'I know she was part of what got Rob killed.'

'You don't know that. Look, I'm telling her I can't talk now, OK. I just felt sorry for her.'

'Why?'

'Because . . . I don't know why.' Patrick signed off and closed down his messenger. He could tell from her expression that Becky was still up for a fight. 'Look,' he said, 'she was on the other side of things. She might be able to find out stuff we can't. We don't know anything about this Adam Hensel, I thought I might be able to get her to talk.'

'You said you felt sorry for her,' Becky challenged, unconvinced.

'That too, I guess.'

'And have you found out anything?' Charlie wanted to know.

'Give me a chance. I've only spoken to her twice.' This was not exactly the truth. Twice implied maybe brief conversations. In fact the second one had lasted a couple of hours and, to Patrick's discomfort, neither Rob nor Adam had been mentioned much. It had been as though both he and Jennifer danced around the subject, avoiding it consciously whenever anything impinged. They'd talked about college and music and films and even Jen's baby and how scared she was. Patrick found that part hard to get his head around. He'd found himself saying all the comforting and reasonable things he knew his nan or Naomi would say under the same circumstances and it had been weird, recycling good advice that was only nominally his. Jennifer had seemed to appreciate it though and, to his surprise, he had warmed to her. 'If I get to talk later on I'll find out what's happening their end,' he promised.

Charlie shrugged. 'Any intel is useful,' he said.

'Intel!' Becky was scornful. 'What the hell are you? Some

sort of spook?' She cast Patrick another suspicious look. 'Don't feel too sorry,' she warned. 'It's Rob we're interested in, not some girl stupid enough to get herself pregnant.'

Patrick shrugged, unsure of what to say. They left soon after, revision demands and the knowledge that they were maybe not as prepared as they should have been pressing down on them. Patrick was left alone. Harry still not home and the house creaking as the central heating warmed its joints unnerved him, even though he knew the source.

He glanced at the time, Harry wouldn't be long. He raced downstairs to the kitchen and filled the kettle, leaving the lights on in the hall and living room even though he had no plan to be there. He and Harry usually shared the cooking once his father was home and, though Patrick might grumble, he actually enjoyed that bit of winding down time and the idle chat that usually accompanied it. Harry would complain about his boring day in the accounts department and talk about the oddities of the staff he worked with. Patrick would complain about his teachers, the homework they'd set, the petty injustices of school and what they'd watch on television that night.

Not overwhelmingly exciting, perhaps, but it was secure and ordinary and Patrick liked it. Comparing his home life to that of Becky – her mother and *him* – or even Charlie, with three siblings to compete with, Patrick counted himself luckier than most. Not that he was always keen on telling Harry that.

Leaving the kettle to boil, he went back upstairs to see if Jennifer was still online. She had already gone. He thought about the conversation he had overheard between Alec and Naomi and the mysterious informant in Pinsent. He'd tackle his dad about that later tonight, make out he knew more than he did and tease Harry into filling in the gaps – a game Harry was more adept at winning these days, Patrick noted wryly.

He wondered about telling Jennifer. It was obvious from what he could piece together that Adam had been seeing someone disreputable and that someone was probably a prostitute. Should he mention it to her, ask her to find out more?

He rejected the notion almost as the thought completed.

He didn't now her that well, did he. What could he say? Hey, was your uncle paying for sex? Maybe you could ask your mum or dad, see if they know. Yeah. Right. Besides, he actually quite liked Jennifer and had no wish to crush the embryonic friendship before it began.

The sound of Harry's key in the door and his father's shout put it all from his mind. He raced downstairs into the brightly lighted hall.

Jennifer had been disappointed when Patrick had cried off. Life at her grandfather's house was quiet. Too quiet and she was seriously bored. She'd waited all day for someone to talk to and when Patrick had appeared online, earlier than usual, it had seemed like a Godsend.

Then he'd made some excuse and logged off. It didn't seem fair.

She almost wished she was back at school. She was due to go to that centre thing next week, she remembered. The place for pregnant teens that was supposed to keep them on track with their lessons.

'Some hope,' Jennifer muttered, half wishing she had actually done the work her form tutor kept sending her. After all, she could access all the handouts through the college intranet and get essay advice too should she need it. It had all seemed like too much stress and a big waste of time, but now, she began to wonder what she was actually going to do. A seventeen-year-old with a baby in tow. She'd kind of hoped her mother would take over but Beth had made it clear that, while they would be supportive, *she* was the mother and had to make the decisions regarding the baby. Her family wanted her to finish her education. The support worker she had seen had told her this was perfectly possible. Patrick, in their last conversation, had pointed out that it might be a good idea . . . and she was coming round to the thought that it might just be.

She flopped down on the bed and stared up at the elaborately corniced and moulded ceiling, one hand resting on her swollen belly. Would parental support be withdrawn, now she was persona non grata in her own house? The surge of resentment she felt towards her mother was tempered only by the reluctant acknowledgement that she'd screamed just as loud and that Grandfather Ernst was right. She should have waited for a better, more opportune moment to reveal her little secret.

If her mother hadn't been so picky that morning – Jennifer could no longer recall exactly what about – she would never have reacted in that way. So, it was her mother's fault. And, she obviously didn't care. She hadn't phoned or anything.

OK, so her dad had called and Jennifer refused to speak to him and Ernst had told him best to let her stew – Jennifer wasn't supposed to have heard that part. She'd stormed out of the room, but not completely out of earshot. He hadn't, to her knowledge, called back again.

Privately, Jennifer had to admit she'd stewed enough. She waned to go home, to have her own things around her and her mother fussing, her father looking bemused, the baby things organized.

Patrick, she thought, he might understand, if he could find the time to actually talk to her! Rob would have understood. So would Uncle Adam. She missed them both and felt traitorous for doing so.

Or did she? Did she really miss Uncle Adam? While a big part of her said yes to that, terrible as it might sound, there was just a little niggling doubt in her mind, some small element that said 'no'; it was, almost, a relief that he was no longer there.

Twenty-Eight

E rnst had returned to his son's flat. The echoing emptiness of the place struck him as soon as he walked through
the door. The furnishings might still be in place, the personal
effects still intact, but the spirit that inhabited it had gone.
It was just a series of rooms and no longer made pretence
at being a home.

He switched the computer on and entered the password at
the prompt. Suzanne was right, he thought as he noted which
version of Windows Adam was running. Although the case
might be the same, the innards of the machine had almost
certainly been upgraded. It surprised him. It was the kind of
thing his son would have told him about, probably finding
some reason for complaint regarding the service or the cost
when he obtained the parts. It was the sort of random, un-
important, factual information that Adam would have felt
safe and found easy to exchange.

Had their relationship so diminished, Ernst wondered, that
now they only discussed the technical, the abstract, the
impersonal? With a jolt he realized that on this occasion
Adam had chosen not even to share in that.

Surely there had been more to it? Reprising the last few
conversations they had shared, Ernst had been forced to
acknowledge that there was probably not. The meetings had
been enjoyable enough, but had been gatherings of the family,
not chat between father and son. The talk had been of family
in general terms and then turned on to politics and film and
the soap operas Beth liked to watch and Adam ridiculed.

Was that what family life was like?

Ernst thought about his time with Lisle. They had been
able to talk about anything, but, he reflected, there had also

141

been many hours spent in silence, comfortable and comforting or in chat about nothing at all. Perhaps he was sifting though his bank of memories looking for problems that did not exist; absences that were in fact not even that. After all, what did he and Adam really have in common bar the accident of birth and fatherhood, and didn't Adam make a point of attending family gatherings? Keeping the contacts and connections alive and active?

After all, Ernst told himself irritably, life does not comprise only of deep and meaningful experiences; much of it is quite banal. Why should conversation and interaction between father and son differ from that?

Reluctantly, feeling that he was intruding into his dead son's privacy, he began to examine the folders and files. Adam was meticulous here as well. In a folder marked 'Correspondence' were letters of complaint to his bank; to his credit card company querying a payment; to his solicitor; his ex-wife; random colleagues . . . going back roughly five years. Each had been subdivided into separate nested folders complete with headings. Ernst scanned them. Nothing that stood out.

There was a folder marked 'Accounts' which contained just that. Adam, in addition to his day job as a surveyor, did some consultancy work and declared it for tax separate from his normal work. There was a folder relating to work and another containing random articles he seemed to have downloaded.

Downloaded? Ernst examined the physical machine more closely. Plugged into a port at the rear was a cable he had not seen. It was coiled and bound with a metal twist tie to keep it tidy, then tucked beneath the tower unit out of the way. Adam had always hated dangling cables.

On the wall behind, hidden behind the table was an extension socket for the phone.

Adam used the Internet? Of course he did, at work, but Ernst had always been under the impression that work was where it ended. He supposed, as Adam did some of his consultancy work from the flat, it made sense to have at least dial up for email, but he had never mentioned it and none of the bills Ernst had seen seemed to relate – though, of course, he'd not looked that closely and a dial up service would be recorded as a number not necessarily listed as an ISP.

Ernst turned his attention back to the folders, skimming through the articles all of which seemed related to surveying, architecture or design. Then on to the next one which contained family photos. Adam had bought a digital camera a year or so before, Ernst recalled and now he took to recording every gathering for posterity. Weddings and Christmases and summer picnics. Some of the better pictures he had printed out at the local supermarket – he said it was hardly worth buying a dedicated printer – and now rested in albums, some in Ernst's own.

He had expected the next folder to be more of the same and so it seemed at first, with a file marked 'Jennifer' nested inside. And one bearing the designation Angel. Curious, Ernst opened that first.

Angel could be termed an attractive woman, Ernst supposed. She certainly seemed eager to show off her attributes, some of which Ernst guessed had been artificially enhanced. The images were no more explicit that those you could find in a daily paper, but Ernst was still astonished by their presence.

Hesitantly, he clicked on the other file, then shut it down. The background told him that the shots of Jennifer had been taken here, in this room and there was no doubt either that she had seen the images of Angel, the poses copied shot for shot.

Ernst felt shaken to the core.

Patrick had returned to the files from Rob's computer but, frankly, he was bored. Nothing exceptional had yet appeared and nothing terribly interesting either. Patrick could remember doing a lot of these essays himself and the fact that Rob had completed the tasks at greater length and with more accomplished spelling really didn't add to their attractiveness.

Tenacious though, he continued to work methodically through the files. Slowly, he began to realize that not all was as it seemed. Rob, as Charlie had commented earlier, certainly was in need of a good clear out. The GCSE syllabus had been roughly the same when he had taken it as when Patrick had the following year. From Patrick's point of view, one of the saving graces of the exam board the college used was that it allowed a percentage of the marks to be derived from coursework. A folder of work was marked alongside the formal exam and it was this that had enabled Patrick to just scrape a bare pass. His folder, written and rewritten under Naomi's guidance, had been better than he either expected or deserved. He'd actually been quite proud of it and, clearing his own computer ready for the new academic year, it had been one of the few things he had chosen to keep.

Rob's folder, of course, was there alongside all the other detritus and Patrick, who had struggled to make the minimum word count with his own compositions, was surprised at how much Rob had crammed inside. Then he looked more closely, examining the titles of the individual compositions, and he knew he was on to something.

True, the syllabus and demands for the work in the folder changed a little year on year, but the basic framework remained the same: the Shakespeare essay, the one comparing poets, the free composition about a place you'd visited . . . Patrick was familiar with these and the random assortment of other work he'd polished up as makeweights. Rob, even allowing for the fact that he found this easy and generally wrote more than Patrick ever could, nevertheless had articles in his folder that had no logical right to be there.

Patrick began to open the unfamiliar ones. One began:

A girl called Jennifer lived until she was seventeen never knowing that she had a brother. They had been separated soon after birth, just like the characters in the fairy tales, and brought up in different parts of the tiny kingdom. Jennifer was rich while her brother was poor and the woman who raised him as her son worked all hours to scrape a living. And all the time they were growing up, although they didn't know about each other, each one had the strangest feeling that there was something missing. It was like knowing you should have an extra hand, even though everyone else told you how stupid that would be when you mentioned anything about it.

Patrick stared, understanding what Rob had been about in writing this. What Rob did with words Patrick did with his drawings: he tried hard to make some kind of sense of the world; to beat it into submission with paint or pen and make it manageable. Solvable.

Patrick checked the date this had been written, closing the file and holding his mouse over it. July. Rob had added this to the folder in July.

Twenty-Nine

It had been agreed that Jennifer should go home. The atmosphere in the house that morning when Ernst had visited his daughter was such that a rime of frost covered the dust free furniture. But she was calming down. Ernst had told her the full story as he knew it, of Rob and Clara and the circumstances of Jennifer's meeting.

He left, feeling that she was likely to be quicker forgiving Jennifer than him. Jennifer, she could classify as young and stupid – and with plentiful evidence, in Beth's eyes, to support that belief – and she would be more likely to blame herself for her daughter's mistakes than Jennifer herself. Ernst had no illusions that this was a healthy state of affairs, but he figured it was inevitable and therefore neither worth his time nor effort to fight.

Ernst himself, she would treat with icy disdain far beyond the spring thaw. He calculated it might well be midsummer before the chill lessened and in his heart, he couldn't blame her. It weighed heavy on him that he might be the bearer of still more bad news, that the winter of the soul could only deepen should he reveal what he had found on Adam's computer.

He had been up all night thinking but the dawn had brought no clarity and his conversation with Beth only deepened his indecision. For all their differences, Beth had adored her elder brother and he was loath to deliver more pain to her door. He thought about confronting his granddaughter with the evidence and demanding an explanation, but held back. Ernst himself was still considering what all this meant. He was unready for the exposure; unprepared for the implications, though he knew that he could not altogether hide his anxiety from Jennifer and that she would probably misconstrue the distance that had seemed to have appeared, chasm like, since the night before.

The photographs could, he thought, have some logical and innocent explanation but he was hard pressed to think of one and he had still not quite put into words what the most likely reason for Adam having such pictures might be. His thoughts had played around the periphery of this all night, reaching out, half grasping the nettle, then pulling back.

He piled Jennifer's bags into the boot of the car, convinced she had more now than she had arrived with. The bulk, he thought, was most likely made up of glossy magazines. He'd had no concept that so many existed aimed at young women. Lisle had occasionally bought one or other of the weeklies, liking the stories and the recipes, but a swift glance through these revealed neither: sex, fashion, music and more sex, oh and a great wedge of problem pages. Was this the intellectual fodder upon which girls Jennifer's age habitually grazed?

Yesterday he would have been amused; yesterday he *had* been amused. Today, he regarded the glossy, garish publications with a more jaundiced eye. Today a world that had slowly been regaining the colours lost the day that his son died, had reverted to monotone, and even the chill, watery sun failed to lift his mood.

'Jennifer,' he began. *Jennifer, was your uncle Adam . . .* 'Jennifer, the father of your baby. Was he . . . is he someone we might know. The family might know?'

She looked puzzled and shrugged her shoulders. He knew she was nervous about returning home. Nervous and trying hard to be offhand. Her answer reflected that mood. 'What's the matter, Granddad? You afraid of what the neighbours might think?'

He could see from her face, from the way she looked away and swallowed hard that she regretted her words as soon as they were out. They were unfair and unreasonable. Another time he might have chided her, gently told her how hurtful that was and elicited an apology and a smile. A hug and a plea for forgiveness. But he didn't seem to have the patience for that today. He could tell that Jennifer was hurting more even than he was, that her barbed words pierced her more deeply, but he needed the harshness to keep the questions and the fears at bay.

When he finally dropped her at her mother's house, the ten-minute journey seeming to take three times as long, she took her bags and stalked into the house, not even pausing to say goodbye.

Thirty

At first Clara didn't recognize the rather portly man who knocked on her door, then when he spoke, it dawned on her.

'Hell, Clara,' he said. 'I had to come and see you.'

'James? Jamie Scott?' She couldn't believe it. Where was the skinny, dark haired teenager she had known? This man, thinning on top and dressed in belted jeans that he had chosen should go under his belly because, presumably, they wouldn't fit over the top, was not the James she remembered.

To be fair, the years had passed for her too, but, as she closed the door and caught a glimpse of herself in the hall mirror, her years had been a darn sight kinder.

'Why are you here? For that matter, how did you find me?'

'I went and asked your mother. She's still at the old place. She gave me your address. I would have called first, but I thought, you know, make it more of a surprise.'

More of a shock, Clara thought, than a surprise.

'And you wanted to see me, why?'

He was taken aback. 'Well, I thought that was obvious.'

'Not to me. No.' She sighed. OK, let the man say his piece, then she'd at least have the satisfaction of knowing she'd been fair. Though what he had to say to her after all this time she couldn't comprehend.

'OK,' she said reluctantly. 'I'll make you a coffee, you can say your piece and then you can go.'

'Don't be like that, Clara. Don't I deserve more than that after all we shared?'

'Whatever little we shared was almost two decades ago.'

He looked crestfallen. 'Well, I suppose I expected more of a welcome,' he admitted. 'But, all right,'

149

He flapped flabby arms against his sides reminding her of a penguin. No, he was too fat to be a penguin. *They* were streamlined. He was more like one of those big seals.

'Coffee it is then and a nice chat. Between friends.'

She showed him through to the living room and told him to sit down, then went through to the kitchen and used the time it took to boil the kettle to gather her thoughts. She'd already decided he only deserved instant coffee and, after a further moment, she searched in the cupboard for the cheap supermarket stuff she kept for making cakes. What right had this flabby man to come here, to go and see her mother, to expect . . .? What exactly did he expect?

She carried the coffee through and handed him the sugar bowl.

'Oh, no thank you. I'm trying to lose some of this.' He patted the stomach which now hid the belt of his jeans altogether. 'I've been under a lot of strain,' he explained. 'So I've eaten a bit too much lately, I suppose. Still, it'll soon go.'

Did he have some miracle diet up his sleeve? Clara wondered. Or was he planning to deflate? She didn't want to be around if he planned on the second option. Clara, she chided herself. Since when have you been fattist? Clara's sister was a plump woman and it would never have occurred to Clara to have such thoughts as these about her.

He sipped his coffee and, much to Clara's annoyance, seemed to be enjoying it.

He smiled. 'I can't tell you how good it is to see you again and you look so well, especially, considering . . . You never married then? Your mother was telling me.'

'Seeing as I rarely speak to my mother I'm surprised she knows one way or another,' Clara said. 'I never married because my early experience of men taught me they weren't worth the bother.'

She was irritated that he merely clucked his tongue and refused to take offence. 'Women can be just as disappointing, Clara,' he said sententiously. 'I married and look at me.'

You blame your wife for what? Looking like a seal or being a slime ball? Clara, for god's sake you don't know anything about the man. He's as good as a stranger to you.

150

She wondered if she should say something sympathetic, but there was no need for her to bother. Her sympathy was anticipated and assumed and for the next ten minutes Clara sipped her coffee and listened to Jamie Scott wallow. His marriage had been a disaster, his children likewise. He had a lousy job, but other opportunities never seemed to arise. He hated his life and should have stayed with her.

'I would have stood by you, given half the chance,' he assured her.

'Your mother phoned up and told me I was a whore.' So did mine, but that doesn't count.

'I never knew that.'

'I passed you in the street one day and you shouted "scrubber" at me and a few more choice expletives as I remember.'

'I was with my friends, you know how it is. Anyway, I was mad as hell because you'd gone with that Aiden bloke. Can you blame me?'

'Yes, actually. I had sex with Aiden out of spite, because you'd been snogging Maureen Hargreaves. Rumour has it you'd done more than that. Who did you marry in the end anyway?'

'Oh, well, I married Maureen but, like I said, it isn't working out. You and me, though . . .'

'Didn't work out either.' She took a deep breath. The emotional turmoil evoked on seeing this man amazed her. She'd been convinced that she'd put all this aside long ago. Moved on. Now it bubbled from some deep dark pit marked unresolved anger and she couldn't seem to swallow it back down.

Was it really all his fault? Hadn't she been just as foolish? 'Look,' she said in a more conciliatory tone, 'I appreciate the gesture in you coming here, but I really do think you should go. It's been too long and I don't think anything can be gained from raking over old coals, do you?'

His look was pitying. 'I just can't help but think,' he said, 'that if we'd still been together things might have been different. Robert might not have gone off the rails if he'd had a father, a man around.'

151

'A man around?' She blinked, not quite believing what she heard. 'Off the rails. Look,' she shook her head. 'You didn't know Rob and you don't know me. Maybe you should go back to your wife and kids. Be the man for them, huh?'

She stood up, signalling more emphatically that it was time to go, but he sipped his coffee and refused to move. 'Leave,' she said. 'Go now.'

He set the mug down and looked at her with pity in his eyes. It was, she realized with shock, genuine emotion. He had convinced himself of the rightness of what he was saying. Clara couldn't get her head around it, but his next words tipped her over the edge of reason.

'I can understand your grief and how much you resent my not being there for you,' he told her. 'But you should have some sympathy for me as well. After all, Clara. I've lost a son too.'

The next moment he was dripping coffee and yelling about assault. The broken mug lay on the rug.

'Get out,' Clara said. 'Get the hell out of my house.'

Alec's arrival a few minutes later found Clara wiping coffee from the chair and warning him about the damp patch on the rug.

'Oh, sod it,' she said. 'Come through to the kitchen, will you? I can still see that toad of a man sitting in that chair.'

For Alec, she made tea. Properly, in a pot.

'You want to tell me what's happened,' he asked. 'Or do I have to ask which toad?'

She laughed, sat down opposite and poured out, verbatim, what Jamie Scott had said. 'And you know what's worst? I missed with the bloody mug.'

'Maybe just as well,' Alec told her. 'You might have knocked him out and been stuck with him until he came round.' He smiled at her. 'Seriously, are you all right?'

She nodded and got up to pour the tea. 'Oh, bugger. It's got a bit strong, do you mind?'

'No. Like it that way. And that's the first you've seen of him since you got pregnant?'

'Yep. I moved a couple of times. Not far, but far enough

and we just never crossed paths. Amazing what a difference a couple of miles can make. You know, I really didn't recognize him at first. Makes me wonder how much I've changed. You just don't think, do you? You look at your own reflection in the mirror every day and the changes happen little by little and then, it's only when you're confronted by . . . well. It's not a comfortable feeling.'

'You look good,' he said. 'And I don't give out compliments readily.'

'Thanks. I could do with one right now. But I'm being rude. What brings you here? Any developments?'

Alec shook his head. 'It's more of a courtesy call, I'm afraid. The CPS have decided that Rob's personal effects can be released. I came to see if I should bring stuff over. We can hang on to things a while longer if you like. Some families . . . they like to wait.'

Clara shook her head. 'May as well,' she said. 'Charlie phoned me, told me what you'd managed to do with the computer stuff. Charlie wasn't hopeful, but, well, I'm grateful.' She paused. 'They really aren't interested in this any more are they, the police, the CPS, no one. I mean, no one but you.'

Alec shrugged. 'I'm keeping it alive,' he said. 'Best I can. It's down to allocation of resources . . .'

'Of course. I'm sorry the tea's so strong.'

'It's fine. Really.'

'You know, I made him . . .'

'The toad?'

'Yes, the toad. I made him cheap supermarket coffee. How petty is that?'

'Oh, I wouldn't even have given him that, but then, if you hadn't you wouldn't have got to throw it over him.'

'Oh, no. That was mine. Still instant, but decent instant.'

'Now, that was a waste.'

'Can he really accuse me of assault?'

'Technically, yes. But don't worry, he tries anything I'll send the boys round.'

She smiled. 'Thanks,' she said. 'For listening and making me laugh. I need to laugh and yet, I'm afraid to in case

153

anyone sees me. In case they think I'm a bad person, laughing in spite of things. You know, I even close the curtains early when I'm watching television in case someone should think I'm being flippant watching rubbish on the telly. Or they catch me, not crying, not being sad and they think, oh, that dreadful woman. Her son killed a man and then killed himself and there she is, laughing.

'How long is it before you can laugh and it not matter. Is there a rule, a book of etiquette?'

Tears welled, but Alec didn't try to stop her crying. He sat quietly on the other side of the table and waited until the storm burned itself out and then he filled the kettle again and made more tea. 'You can laugh,' he said. 'It's good to laugh and I will personally throw cheap supermarket coffee over anyone who dares object.'

Thirty-One

Once they knew what to look for it was so obvious they could not believe they'd missed anything. Apart from a few compositions like the one Patrick had found, the other evidence was hidden within the body of essays and exercises. One essay might have several drafts as Rob revised and saved each one, not choosing to merge the changes but instead saving as a separate file each time. Patrick did something similar with his work, always paranoid about losing something that might actually be better than his revisions.

Where Rob's method differed was that within the earlier drafts he had grafted notes and ideas and names. Information accumulated in the search for his father. Anyone just opening files and scanning would see academic work at various stages. Patrick knew from what Alec said that no one had been assigned to look more closely than this. Alec's taking the computer and books from Rob's home had probably been perceived as almost unnecessary. Rob's guilt had never been in doubt.

Even to Patrick's eyes, these notes seemed random and eclectic. He seemed even to have recorded times when he noticed his mother chatting to sales people in shops. Did she know that man, who was he? Was he anything to do with her past?

It was obsessive and it was weird and it had, judging from the dates these observations had been recorded, been going on for quite some time.

'What was he playing at?' Becky wanted to know. 'It looks like he was spying on people.'

Patrick and Charlie exchanged a glance. They didn't like

the word, but the content certainly led to that conclusion.

'So, what do we do?' Patrick wanted to know. He left his seat at the computer and sat down on the bed, staring accusingly at the screen.

'I think we should tell Alec we couldn't find anything,' Charlie said. 'This is going to make Rob look so bad.'

'Worse than a murderer?' Patrick asked.

'Yeah, kind of.'

Becky took Patrick's vacant seat and began to examine some of the newer files. 'There's a lot about Adam Hensel,' she said. 'And about *her*.'

Patrick assumed she meant Jenny.

'It looks like he followed Adam around,' Becky said. 'This is just one Saturday: "Adam Hensel, 11 a.m at the supermarket. Walks back to flat. 12.30 goes out again in car. 5 p.m home. Jennifer with him."'

'What was he doing?'

Charlie sprawling on Patrick's bed, shrugged. It was clear to Patrick that he wanted shut of this whole thing. Patrick was inclined to agree. 'Look,' he said. 'We either tell Alec we couldn't find anything or we tell him about this and then let the police do the rest. I really don't feel good about it.'

Charlie sat up. 'I agree,' he said. 'What good's this going to do?'

'Us and Clara, we all said we wanted to know why,' Becky objected.

'Yeah, but, we didn't know he'd turn out to be a weirdo.'

'Rob wasn't weird, he was . . .' Becky chewed her bottom lip. She seemed transfixed by the revelations, opening another file and scrolling down.

'Alec would never have set us going on this if he'd thought there'd be this much stuff,' Patrick said. 'He just told me to look for anything that didn't fit.'

'Well, we found that, all right. We struck the motherload of "doesn't fit". Look, I don't want to sound harsh, but I can't deal with all this shit. I've got exams to take and a life and . . . Becks, what's up?'

She got up, grabbed her coat and ran from the room and down the stairs. They heard the front door slam.

'What? Whoa.' Charlie stared at the screen. 'Mate, I'd better go after her,' he said.

Patrick nodded, then went to look at the computer file. 'I like her a lot,' Rob had written. 'I wish she wasn't who she is. My sister and all that. It's like, that Shakespeare thing, you know wherefore art thou and all that. Well, wherefore fucking art thou Jennifer Ryan. Life isn't fucking fair.'

Thirty-Two

A lec looked up at the 1930s block of flats that included the home of the late Adam Hensel. It was a handsome building with a heavy front door set back in an art deco porch. Expensive, Alec thought, and carefully restored to make the most of the original features.

Hensel's name was printed in neat black letters above the bell. Alec hadn't been the one who'd checked out his flat after the murder, and until Ernst had called him an hour ago, not really known where the man had lived.

Ernst released the lock when Alec rang the bell and he found himself in a spacious and airy lobby. The marble floor, though a little scuffed now, and the elaborately panelled walls, reminded Alec of an expensive hotel, an impression enhanced by the presence of a desk like that found in a hotel lobby. Once upon a time there would have been a concierge on duty in the daytime and a night porter, Alec thought. Luxury indeed.

There were two staircases leading off and a lift. Alec chose the stairs. Ernst had told him that the flat was on the second floor and to take the right hand staircase. He arrived, slightly out of breath, to find Ernst standing in the doorway. He looked older, Alec thought, more worn down. He'd looked like that in the days following his son's death, but recently had seemed to recover.

What had happened now to cause such a relapse?

Inside, Ernst led Alec through to the main living room. It was a spacious, well proportioned area with high ceilings and large windows with curiously shaped panes like stretched oblongs. It was dark outside and Alec wondered what the view would be like on a fine day. The flats were high up on a hill almost on the edge of town. On a good day, most like, he'd be able to see Pinsent beach.

The computer was on and Ernst had drawn two chairs close to the oak table.

'Please,' he said. 'Sit down. I have something to show you. I don't want you to see, but, frankly, I don't know what else to do. I have run this problem so many times through my head I feel my brain has absorbed so much it can hold no more. I am run ragged with this.'

'Show me,' Alec said. And Ernst did, bringing up the two files: the one of Angel and the images of Jennifer, posing in only the briefest of bikini bottoms.

Alec said nothing for a moment, then he glanced swiftly round the room.

'Yes, they were taken here.'

'Right. How did you come to find this?'

'I was looking. For answers, I suppose. All I find is questions.' He told Alec how he wanted to look around before the flat was sold. How Suzanna helped him gain access to the computer. How, when he looked again, he found that the machine was more powerful than he had thought. And how he had found these.

'What do I do now? Do I confront Jennifer? Do I tell her mother that Adam . . . that Adam may have had . . .'

'An inappropriate relationship with his niece?'

'Inappropriate. Yes.'

Alec thought hard. 'If Jennifer was sixteen when these were taken and if she gave her full and informed consent, then there may be nothing left to tell. Legally, I mean. It might be . . . inappropriate to take . . . glamour portraits of one's niece, but, providing she was of age and provided she wasn't coerced or pressurized . . .'

'And if she was not?'

'The pictures should be dated. Or, at least, we should be able to find out when they were transferred to the hard drive. Probably both.' He frowned, trying to recall how he'd find out, finally got there. 'August of this year. So she'd be . . .'

'Just turned seventeen, but, Inspector Friedman, even so. This is hardly right. What if. What if . . .?'

159

'Did you find anything to suggest there was more going on?'

Ernst shook his head. 'No, but Inspector,' he took a deep breath, 'she became pregnant not so long after that. What if. What if Adam was the father?'

There, he'd said it and the heavens hadn't opened and struck him down. Vaguely, Ernst realized he'd almost expected them to.

'She was still of age. Yes, there would be the question of two close blood relatives . . . not to mention the moral questions surrounding any relationship where one partner is so much younger, but . . .' He sighed. 'The thing that occurs to me as well, and I'm sure must have occurred to you; what if Jennifer told Rob about this? What if Rob decided Adam had seduced or coerced? That would give us additional motive for him attacking your son. Perhaps, the whole motive.'

Ernst nodded again. 'Do I talk to her?' he asked. 'What do I say?'

'I think we have to,' Alec said, choosing to share responsibility with this shocked and anguished old man. 'We have to for two reasons at least. We need to know what Jennifer told Rob about all this and we need to know too if Adam did have a relationship with her, because if he did, with them being such close kin, the child's welfare becomes a paramount question. And we need to know for a third reason. Ernst, you'll never rest easy until you're sure, one way or another. Grief on top of grief can wear you down until there's nothing left.'

It was late, Harry was thinking about bed. He'd been surprised at Patrick's friends leaving separately and Patrick not coming down to say goodbye. Had they quarrelled?

He made them both hot chocolate, frothing it in the special pot Mari had given him at Christmas. Mari knew how he loved his kitchen gadgets. He stood at the foot of the stairs with both mugs on a tray, wondering whether he should call Patrick down or take his mug upstairs. Instinct induced him to take both mugs and to go up to his son's room.

He knocked.

160

'Come in, Dad.'

Patrick was drawing, using the new pens Harry had bought him. He'd been delighted with them as Naomi said he would be. Harry had, at the time, thought it was an odd sort of gift and an expensive one considering they were only glorified felt tips.

'Good, are they?'

Patrick nodded. 'Brilliant. Thanks.' He looked up and eyed the mugs. 'Frothy chocolate?'

'Frothy chocolate.'

Patrick grinned and for an instant looked about eight years old again. Such a barrel of contradictions, Harry thought. 'I wondered if you wanted to come down for it.'

Patrick shook his head. 'No, but Dad, sit down a minute?'

It was unusual to be invited to stay in Patrick's domain. Harry sat, placing the tray beside the computer.

'These are good,' he was genuinely surprised. 'How do you grade the tone like that?'

'That's what the pens are designed for. It's easy to keep the wet edge moving.' He demonstrated. 'See, you don't get lines and every colour will blend or overlay the others.'

Harry studied the images more closely. The comic book style came naturally to his son. Graphic novel, he corrected himself. He had to confess too that, though he might once have been dismissive of such things, his son had taught him that there was a real art to the storytelling and to the pared down graphic style. It wasn't his thing, but, he admitted, there were skills involved.

'Is this Rob?' he asked gently.

'Yeah. Look Dad, I know you might think it's a bit macabre, but . . .'

'Does it help you cope? With his death, with the other stuff you're going through?'

Patrick hesitated, and then nodded. 'It's like, I can make it happen to someone else, not to my friends and me. It's like I can kind of make it into a story. It hurts, but it makes it further away. Does that make any sense?'

Harry nodded. 'I think so. Yes.'

Patrick made a grab for his chocolate and nearly upset the

161

mug. He had always tended towards the clumsy but his awkwardness magnified when he was upset.

'These new ones. What are they about?'

Patrick hesitated then pushed the stack of drawings towards his father. His manner warned Harry that he must be careful what he said, that Patrick was expecting a reaction; it had to be the right one. Harry slowly worked his way through the stack. The illustration was swiftly done and the pictures followed one from the other. He cleared a space and laid them out upon the table. Rob again, standing toe to toe with another man. His back was to the viewer and his shoulders hunched. 'Adam Hensel,' Harry said.

The next picture showed Rob backing off, his gestures spoke of irritation, even desperation and the other man was turning now as though to walk away.

In the third, it was clear that something had gone wrong. Harry spaced it so that a missing picture would fit in the space. He heard his son release held breath and knew he'd guessed right. This was the point at which Patrick was at a loss. He couldn't work it out. The next image showed Adam Hensel with a knife clutched in his hand. Harry knew that the actual weapon had been a folding pocket knife, but in Patrick's pictures, the blade was long, vicious, brutal and it glinted in the light from the street lamp Harry now saw featured in all of the designs. Another gap and the knife was in Rob's hand. Hensel lay at his feet and the look on Rob's face was one of shock, horror, sheer despair. His son had captured the emotion of the moment so vividly, done so with a few strokes of the pen that Harry was at the one time moved by the strength of it and awed at his skill.

'You really are good,' he said.

'Thanks, Dad,' Patrick said. 'But I still don't know why or how it really happened. But we found something. In Rob's computer stuff.'

Harry sensed that he'd passed some test in the last few minutes. That, probably without realizing it himself, his son had been waiting to see if he could be trusted with something else he couldn't work out and didn't understand.

'What did you find?'

162

Patrick squeezed his lips together in a long flat line. He looked pinched and tired and in the harsh light of the desk lamp his hair seemed very black, his skin unearthly pale.

'We think Rob was stalking Adam Hensel,' he said. 'And he'd been doing it for a while. And, Adam Hensel wasn't the only one.'

Thirty-Three

Aiden was at work, Beth preparing to leave for her part time job and Jennifer still in bed when Ernst arrived with Alec following close behind. Ernst had printed out the pictures at Alec's suggestion. They felt that confronting Jennifer with the indisputable evidence might be a shock tactic that would jolt more truth from her than the softly softly approach everyone had tried so far.

'Dad, what's going on?' Beth wanted to know.

'Call work,' Ernst told her. 'You'll be late today.'

'I'll be . . . don't be silly. Why should I be late?'

'I have some questions to ask your daughter,' Alec told her quietly. 'You need to be here.'

Beth was about to argue further but thought better of it. 'Oh what now,' she muttered. 'What else is bloody wrong with this family.' She phoned her job, went to get Jennifer out of bed. Ernst made tea in the kitchen and a bleary eyed, dressing gown clad teenager arrived protesting, her mother in tow, a few minutes later.

Alec noted that Beth made no move to invite them into the lounge. She was obviously seething, preparing for the next round of battles. Silently, Alec laid the prints out on the table.

The silence thickened as the two women studied them. Then Jennifer tried to get in first. 'Mum, I can explain. It isn't what you think.'

'How the hell,' Beth said slowly, 'can you possibly know what I think?' She jabbed a finger at the offending pictures. 'What are these? Dad, Inspector, just what the hell are these? And you, you'd better have a bloody good story.'

'I do,' Jennifer protested, but she was struggling, drowning,

164

eyes darting looking for a means of escape, of relief. 'I do, honestly I do.'

'These were on Adam's computer,' Ernst said.

'On what?' Beth turned on him throwing her hands in the air. 'Oh, now I've heard it all. What is this, some kind of smear campaign? My brother was murdered. Have you forgotten that? What? Does that make him fair game for every rumour, every accusation, every bloody . . .'She turned back to Jennifer. 'So,' she said. 'And what explanation do you reckon you have that's so damned good?'

Jennifer looked away, her blonde hair fell across her face and Alec could not read her expression.

'Did Adam take them?' Ernst asked her.

She nodded.

'Adam? Oh for heaven's sake. Adam would never.'

'Then,' Alec asked Beth, 'how come they turned up on his machine?'

'How should I know? Maybe you lot planted them there. You seem so keen to blame the bloody victim here and that's what he was, don't you forget. That little shit murdered my brother. He stabbed him with his own knife and he ran away and then he killed himself, so I don't even have the satisfaction of seeing him rot in jail.'

'Rob wasn't like you think.' Jennifer's head was up, her cheeks flaming. 'Rob was kind and nice and he wanted, wanted . . .'

Beth hit out. She couldn't help herself. It was all too much. Her fingers raked her daughters face and then she stood, horrified at what she'd done but shaking and staring as though she'd like to do it all over again.

'Beth!'

'Mrs Ryan!'

Jennifer leapt to her feet overturning the chair and ran from the room. Beth sank back into her chair and buried her face in her hands.

'I'd better go,' Ernst headed for the door. 'Lord, what a mess this is.'

Alec waited until the crying had almost ceased. It seemed to be his week for weeping women. He found a roll of kitchen towel and nudged her hand. She lifted her head slightly and, reluctantly, took the towel. Wiped her eyes and blew her nose.

'He's right you know,' Alec said. 'It is a mess. A big mess and we have to sit down like sensible adults and sort it out.'

'Jennifer isn't a sensible adult.'

'No, she's not, she's a scared seventeen-year-old. We have to be adult for her as well.'

'You sound like you think *I'm* behaving like a kid,' she spat at him.

'No, I don't, but I think you have to wake up to the fact that your brother may not have been purer than the driven snow. He took those pictures, they were taken in his flat and even if that was all that happened, it was . . . well, at best unwise. You must see that?'

Beth stared miserably at the pictures. 'What the hell did she think she was doing?'

'No. What the hell did either of them thing they were doing? Adam was the adult here. Even if it was some kind of semi-innocent prank, he should still have put the brakes on.'

He waited, wondering if he should tell her about Angel, decided now was as good a time. 'Jennifer was copying poses,' he said. 'From some pictures Adam already had on his computer. A young woman who calls herself Angel. We believe Adam was seeing her.'

'Adam had a girlfriend? She posed for pictures. I mean that's not so . . .'

'No. Angel wasn't Adam's girlfriend. Adam . . . paid her. She's an escort, a prostitute.'

'No! Adam wouldn't.' She stared at Alec. 'Jesus, how much more sordid can all this get?'

'I don't know,' Alec told her honestly. 'I really couldn't say.'

Ernst sat on the top step outside Jennifer's door. He could hear her sobbing. Angry, aching, self-pitying sobs that made him want to slap her and comfort her all at the same time. Beth, he figured, must be feeling the same, though the more

166

violent impulse had momentarily won out over the maternal one.

'Jen darling, talk to me.'

'I don't want to talk to anyone. She hit me.'

'And she's sorry.'

'No, she's not. She's a bitch. She hates me. She's hated me for a long time. Uncle Adam never liked her. She was just jealous of him and me.'

Ernst felt his stomach tighten. He forced himself to stay calm. 'Jennifer, my love, come and talk to me. You have to talk to me.'

'No, I don't. I don't have to talk to anyone.'

'Why did he take the pictures? Was it a game?'

'Game! Like I'm a kid.'

The door opened and she came out. Her face was red, but Ernst doubted it would bruise too much. She had anticipated the blow and ducked backwards even as her mother lashed out at her. 'If not a game, then what?'

'I don't know. He liked me. He said I was pretty.'

'And you are.'

'Huh. Not now I'm not. Look at me. Fat and shapeless. I'll probably be like that forever now.'

'No, you won't. You'll get your figure back after the baby. It won't take long.'

'But then I'll be saddled with it, won't I? My life's over, Granddad.'

He slid an arm around her shoulders and hugged her tight. 'No, no it's not. You'll go back to your studies and you'll get a good job, maybe go to university. There are nurseries and crèches for the little one.'

'Mum thinks I should look after it.'

'And so you should. But not on your own and not to the exclusion of everything else. There are ways of dealing with this, Jennifer. Besides, when it's born, you'll love it. I told you that. Then it won't seem so hard. Now, talk to me because I need to know. Why did Adam take the pictures? Hey?'

She shrugged. 'Because I asked him to.'

'You asked him to?'

167

'I was round at his place and he gave me some wine and we cooked a meal and he said I'd suddenly got very grown-up and very pretty and we got giggly and a bit silly, I suppose and he showed me these pictures on his computer of this woman and he said I was prettier than her and he took my pictures. And afterwards I woke up with a hangover and he promised he'd erased them. He broke his promise, Granddad. Why did he do that?'

'Hush now, darling. I don't know why. Maybe he forgot. Maybe.'

He kissed her hair and hugged her even tighter. 'Jennifer, I have to ask this. Did anything else happen while you were there?'

'You mean, did we have sex.' Irritably, she pulled away.

'Yes, I mean that. Jennifer, it's important. Did you then, or any other time?'

She shrugged, not looking at him, hiding again behind the fall of blonde hair. 'I don't know,' she said finally. 'Maybe. I just don't know.'

Thirty-Four

Harry had phoned in and asked for a half day's holiday, something he'd never done at the last minute before. It was a measure of his concern for his son that he had done so now. He turned up at Naomi's flat while she was having breakfast.

'I've got something to read to you,' he said. 'Can you spare a few minutes?'

'Sure. What's the trouble?'

'Rob Beresford, I would say.'

'Patrick and his friends found something.'

'Patrick did. The others freaked, as they say, when they started to uncover truths they didn't like.'

'Understandable. What do you have?'

She made more tea and fresh toast for Harry while he read from the printouts, starting with the one about Jennifer and her lost brother. He moved on to the notes Rob had kept about Adam's movements. Finished with some of Rob's observations on the friends his mother met, her work colleagues, the grocer down the street.

'And there's more,' he told her.

'Wow.'

'Yes, that's pretty much what I thought. Patrick wasn't sure what to do. I told him we had to speak with Alec. We talked about this for a long time last night.'

'I can imagine. Good that you talked though.'

'Good that we talked. Do you realize how talented my son is? What an amazing artist? No, how could you? I'm sorry, I forgot there for a moment.'

'Actually,' Naomi said, 'I do. Patrick tells me a lot about what he's doing. Harry, I may not be able to see the finished work, but I know what he feels about it. I know how committed he is and I believe you that he's good.'

'I never looked before. I thought, oh yes, it's all right, let him do it, get his qualifications, then talk to him about life getting serious and the need to get a job and all that ordinary stuff.' He laughed. 'I'm only glad I didn't get to do it.'

'Patrick will do just fine,' Naomi said. 'He's just never going to be an accountant.'

'Lucky him.'

'It's not too late to do something else.'

'Hmm, well, that's a discussion for another time. I don't hate it; I just don't like it that much, that's all. Anyway, what do we do about this stuff?'

'We talk to Alec. I think it'll have to be his call. What do you want on your toast?'

They chatted for a time over breakfast, but the conversation spiralled round to the same subject again.

'You know, while you're here, you can do something for me.'

'Of course. What do you have in mind?'

'Well, you remember Jodie, the woman you took me to see in Pinsent.'

'Not easily forgotten.'

'Well, she came up with a lead. A woman who calls herself Angel, though actually her name's Angela. Anyway, Adam Hensel was one of her clients. It seems he also used her website. She gave me the address, but I've not had a chance to see what's on it yet. Alec got a call and had to go and,' she laughed, 'I thought you might draw the line at Patrick helping on that kind of job.'

'Hmm, yes I would rather. You're telling me this is a . . . er . . . pornography site?'

'Well, more of a peep show, I believe. But don't worry, we won't be able to get in that far. It's a subscription site, though we know that Adam was a regular subscriber. All I want to know, Harry, is what the site looks like, and Angel too. You could say it's idle curiosity on that front.'

Harry took a deep breath. 'All right,' he said. 'In for a penny. What do I have to do?'

170

'Read what it says here when I tell you.' She handed him the slip of paper upon which Angel had written her web address, then fired up her machine and waited for the screen prompt beep Patrick had set up for her. Then she switched on the microphone. 'Internet.'

'I say. You can talk to it now?'

'Search.' She covered the microphone. 'Can you read the web address to me?' She listened, then repeated it into the microphone.

'Wouldn't it be quicker if I do that?'

'I doubt it. It's voice recognition software. Took me an age to train the blasted thing. Patrick's registered as a second user and he's pretty good. Though I still make him type his essays.'

'Oh, I think we're in,' Harry said.

'OK, you take over with the mouse.' She switched off the microphone and vacated her seat. 'What do you see?'

'Um. Well, there's a young woman in a bikini doing exercises in the middle of the screen and various options I can click on around that. One is for vitamin supplements. One is for Life Coaching. What's that when it's at home? And there are exercise routines. Then there's the members only section.'

'OK, have a play, click on some of the options and see where they take you.'

'Oh, all right. Now let me see.' For the next half hour they played around on the site, discovering 'The Herbal Alternative to Viagra' and exercises that promoted sexual harmony between partners. Harry was amused and slightly shocked. 'You know,' he said, 'I don't believe you can really do that. It must be trick photography.'

'Do what?'

'Well, she's sort of lying on her back with one leg straight up and the other one out to the side and her hand is sort of . . . um, well. One is up by her head and the other is reaching round. No, you can't . . . '

'Want to try?'

'Naomi, I was never that supple, not even when I was young and slim.'

171

'When who was young and slim?' Alec said.

'Oh hello. We didn't hear you. What are you doing here at this time of day?'

'I'm not surprised you didn't hear me. I can hear the pair of you down the hall, giggling like a pair of schoolgirls. What am I missing? Oh, that's what I'm missing. Our sweet Miss Angel.'

He kissed Naomi. 'God, what a morning. I needed a break and I need tea and this is better than the canteen. Anyone want to join me?'

'Harry has something for you. Patrick found some stuff on Rob's computer.'

Over tea and yet more toast, they exchanged information. Alec allowing Harry in on what had been going on in the Hensel household and knowing it would go no further.

'Do you think he was the father?' Naomi asked.

'I'm not so sure. Neither am I sure they didn't have sex. Jennifer swears she can't remember and apparently it was quite a common thing for her to stay over at her uncle's place. My feeling is, Adam took the pictures when they'd both had too much to drink, pretty much as Jennifer said. That she did think he'd erased them. I also got the impression things were getting a bit too heavy for her. Maybe it went further, maybe she was afraid it might.'

'Or that it might not?'

'That too. Who knows? Unless Jennifer clarifies the situation there's not a great deal anyone can do, but these latest revelations haven't exactly smoothed familial relations chez Ryan.'

'So, what happens next?' Harry wanted to know.

'With Jennifer or Patrick?'

'Either, both.'

'Jennifer . . . who knows? Ernst will keep me in the loop, that's if Beth keeps him in the loop. Patrick? He's done a good job. Harry, I hate to involve him more than I have to but if you could help him compile a list of everyone Rob was interested in, I can take it to Clara. That way, we might be able to find out just how deep this obsession went and if he had any other near misses in the past. I can't think Adam Hensel was the first person who noticed him hanging around.'

Thirty-Five

That afternoon Alec called Ernst. 'How are you?' Alec asked.

'Tired. But I can't seem to sleep. If anything I feel worse now than I did in the days after he died. Alec, can I ask you to drop this. I don't want to find out anything more. I just want to let things lie.'

'I can understand that. Look, Ernst, I'll involve you and your family as little as possible from now. I promise that.'

'I appreciate the sentiment. You'll understand if I don't really believe you. I phoned Suzanna, Adam's ex. I asked her if she remembered any odd behaviour. Sexual behaviour.'

I'll bet that was a fun conversation, Alec thought.

'Suzanna . . . she finally admitted that for the last years of their marriage there was nothing at all. She doesn't know why. It was one of the things that broke their relationship. I . . . told her about the pictures. I needed to know, Alec, if there was ever anything. If she ever suspected anything might be going on between Adam and Jennifer. She was appalled that I should even ask and so am I now. I suppose I should be thankful, when Suzanna divorced Adam, Jennifer would have been only twelve years old. I don't think I could have born it if she'd said yes, she felt there might have been.'

Alec didn't quite know how to respond. He murmured something he hoped was soothing.

'If Jennifer decides to say anything . . .'

'I'll let you know. Oh, Alec, there's something I meant to say. The boy, Patrick.'

'Yes?'

'He was nice to her. The night we all met at Clara's he said she should get in touch if she wanted to talk. He wrote

174

something for her on a little slip of paper. Not a phone number. Perhaps his email. He felt sorry for her, I think, but he was kind.'

'Thank you,' Alec said. 'That's very like the kind of thing Patrick would do. '

He didn't say that he'd ask Patrick what he knew, that Patrick could be as tight mouthed as anyone he knew where confidences were concerned, and he wasn't about to make promises to Ernst on his behalf. But he hoped Patrick would have the sense to realize what should be told if Jennifer did disclose anything new.

He put down the phone feeling oddly drained and ever so slightly soiled.

He thought it was me so I could understand him being angry, but . . . I never did anything. All I wanted was to be friends. He's the one Jen said. Got her that way, took mucky pictures of her even though she was drunk and too out of it to know better. I asked him: That the way you get your kicks is it? But he said nothing, just stood there looking important and I thought I'd just go . . . this was getting us nowhere.

He said, where was I going and I said home and he said, no, no I wasn't not until I'd come back and told them all what I'd done and then I understood it. She'd told him. Told him one thing and me another and we'd both believed her and I got mad then. With her, with him, all self righteous when he was the one. Him. And when I looked up the street she was there, all that blonde hair and long legs and everything and she was saying, no, no , I never told him any of that. But I know. Yes, I know.

175

Thirty-Six

Jennifer was on MSN waiting for him when he signed in. Inwardly, Patrick groaned. He felt he could do without this just now, but he tried to be bright and cheerful, mentally telling himself that maybe he should think about blocking her.

Good day?

No lousy. She added an emoticon with a turned down mouth

Oh? Why?

Because my granddad brought me home yesterday and this f***ing policeman turned up with him this morning. That Inspector we met at Clara's place saying all sorts of stuff about Uncle Adam and Mum got upset and she blamed me and said it was all my fault and the rows went on all morning.

'*What sort of bad things?* Patrick was amused by her use of asterisks. Did she think he'd be offended?

Oh Emoticon with upwardly rolling eyes this time. **There were these pictures on his computer, but it was all pretty stupid you know. Mum reckons they're trying to slur his name and he's really the victim and this policeman he was trying to get me to say all these things about Uncle Adam and Mum was throwing a real wobbly and Granddad Ernst just sat there looking sad and it was all a mess.**

Weeping emoticon this time followed by another with rolling eyes.

Patrick knew Alec well enough to read between the lines of what she was saying. Alec would never try to make her say something that wasn't true.

176

Has it all settled down now?

No such luck. Mum is in her room crying again and Dads gone off down the pub though he says he's got some meeting or something but that's down the pub anyway and I'm here on my own. As usual.

It'll all blow over, Patrick soothed. *The police just have a job to do*.

Yeah right and it's making trouble for us all. Why can't they just piss off and leave us alone? Rob's dead and so is Uncle Adam and nothings going to change that. Anyway mums right they just keep dragging up the dirt and they won't stop til were all broken up in little bits.

Patrick felt he had to defend Alec but was pretty sure she wouldn't take any notice anyway. He wanted to ask questions. 'What photographs? What sort of things did you think he wanted you to say?' But Jennifer wasn't going to give him straight answers to any of those things so what was the point? Anyway, he wasn't sure he had the patience to deal with her tonight. He let her rant for a little longer, sending emoticons rather than words in return. She didn't seem to notice that he had so little to say. Finally he told her:

Look I've got homework and it always takes me ages so ive got to get on ok.

Sure right. I'll let you get off then.

She sent another tearful emoticon, just in case he should fail to notice how neglected she now felt and Patrick logged off and shut messenger down. He had no wish to talk to anyone else tonight and the task he had next was not homework exactly but the list Alec had asked him to compile. Patrick wasn't sure he was up to doing it alone. He would, he decided get his dad to give him a hand. Harry's handwriting was so much better than Patrick's anyway and if he could just dictate the names and any addresses and stuff, it would save no end of time.

He flopped back on his bed and stared at the ceiling. A small water stain in the corner, where a loose roof tile had once let in the rain, was bleeding through the last coat of paint Harry had applied. It looked like a mouse, Patrick decided, with something roughly birdlike pecking at its tail.

He could use the shape, take a picture with his digital camera and then play with it in Photoshop. Elements had been another Christmas gift from Harry.

He closed his eyes and his thoughts turned back to Rob, his pond skater friend. The Rob he'd thought of as skimming upon the surface of life it seemed had more legs dangling down into the vicious depths of water than any of them had realized.

He'd been living this double life and none of them had known. Not even Becky had known. Rob had, it seemed, become so skilled at managing both his everyday existence – school, friends, parties, fun – and this other one. Snooping, gathering facts and information. Stalking people. That was what it amounted to.

Patrick shifted restlessly and opened his eyes again to stare at the mouse bird on his ceiling. How long, he wondered, if ever, before he could regain that image of Rob as someone joyful and complete and able to skim across the surface? He had, he realized, counted on their being people like Rob. People whose happy-go-lucky nature he could aspire to, even if he knew it was not his way of being.

Rob, it seemed, was, after all, just another drowning soul.

Thirty-Seven

Clara read through the list of names Alec had brought. She shook her head. 'What is all this?'

'Do you recognize them. Are the names familiar?'

'Um, most, yes. Some of these people I barely know. Ian Henderson . . . I think that's the Mr Henderson at the post office, but I'm not sure. And this man here. I've no idea who Colin Shorter might be.'

Alec checked through the supplementary information Harry and Patrick had given them. Several pages of it; it must have taken hours, he thought guiltily. 'Apparently he's a courier who sometimes delivers stuff you order from a catalogue.'

'I'm sorry?' Clara was mystified. 'So what does he have to do with me? He must deliver and pick up from half the people round here.'

'Probably, but I don't think that mattered to Rob. You had contact with him and that's what counted.'

'I still don't understand.'

'Rob . . . was checking up on people. This list, it's people we found on his computer. Details hidden inside other files and folders. Rob practically stalked Adam Hensel in the weeks before they died.'

'Rob? God, Jennifer said something similar, but I couldn't believe it then and I'm not sure I do now.' She looked to Alec for confirmation, reassurance. 'No. I don't believe that. I don't believe any of it.'

Gently, Alec began to take her through what Patrick and his friends had found. Harry had printed out relevant sections and cross referenced information with names. Or started to. Alec had already realized this was a bigger job than any of them had suspected.

'No,' Clara said again. 'No, I still don't believe it. What was he trying to do?'

'I think,' Alec said, 'that what started out as very natural curiosity became unbalanced, somehow. It tipped over into secrecy and obsession.'

'So you're saying it's my fault. I should have told him who his father might be. I should have noticed something. I should . . .' She broke down. 'When he was a little boy he'd go up to men in the street and ask them, "are you my daddy?". It was embarrassing at the time, but I've known other single parents whose kids have done the same. They grow out of it. They begin to understand that you don't do that sort of thing. I thought Rob had just moved on. Oh, he'd ask from time to time and I knew, when he turned eighteen, I'd have to tell him more.'

'Didn't he ask your family? Your mother? Sister?'

'My sister, yes, but she didn't know anyway. She couldn't, wouldn't tell him anything. My mum. I don't know. I doubt it, we hadn't seen her in years.'

'But he knew where she lived?'

Clara nodded. '*He's* not on the list though. James Scott.'

'No, he's not. Which, considering how thorough Rob seems to have been, surprises me.'

'So it wasn't just Aiden he was trying to make contact with.'

'No, it seems not, but I think events overtook him this time. He got involved with Jennifer and the notes on his computer indicate they'd become very close.'

'And her uncle might have objected?'

'He may have done. There are a number of possibilities, but nothing concrete just now. Clara, there were never any complaints from anyone that Rob was making a nuisance of himself. Hanging round, asking questions.'

She thought about it. Nodded. 'Once, that I can think of, but it was years ago. There was a man came to work in my office and we got to be good friends. He was going through a divorce and for a while we went out, just casually. I even brought him home, though, to be honest, I never thought anything would come of it. He was looking for a bit of company and so was I and a romance would have been nice but . . . The funny thing was, I'd been at school with his sister. She was in my year and we'd been friends, though, you know how it is, you drift off. Anyway, he turned up for work one day and said did I know where Rob had been this weekend. I thought Rob was at his friend's on a sleepover, but he'd spent the Sunday and maybe part of the Saturday as well, hanging round this bloke's house just watching him.

'I tackled Rob and he came out with something about being worried about me seeing as how I was getting a bit close to this guy. He wanted to check him out a bit. I told him off and apologized and it all blew over. Ended the relationship, mind. But Rob was always a bit protective of me and I put it down to that. Far as I know, so did Carl, the man. I think he went back to his wife a few months later anyway and they moved somewhere else to make a fresh start. I often wondered if they managed it.'

She picked up the list. 'He's not on it, anyway.'

'He'd obviously been dismissed. And Rob was, you say, thirteen or so.'

She nodded.

'So, maybe he learnt to be more circumspect after that.'

'So I drove the behaviour underground.'

'Clara, you didn't do anything. Rob got himself into a situation of his own making. But it swallowed him in the end. It probably did start out as idle curiosity and from what I've seen of kids, most of them play detective at one time or another. Rob did it a little more assiduously.'

'But this behaviour wasn't normal. You used the word stalking.'

Alec nodded. 'I think, in Adam Hensel's case, that's what it became. This was probably the best lead Rob had had in a long time. It genuinely seemed to lead somewhere. The trouble was I think the act of doing probably began to over-shadow the reasons behind it and he found himself unable to slow things down. Kids don't always have the ability to make things stop.'

He left Clara with a copy of the list and other information. She had given him addresses for a few of those named

181

and rough indicators for the others. Alec would be able to follow up from the voters' register.

Alec recalled Ernst's plea of the day before. 'Let this drop,' Ernst had said and Alec was tempted to do just that. Hand everything he had discovered over to his boss and leave it up to him whether or not it should be pursued further. After all, what good was he doing? He was only causing more pain to an increasing number of people.

He folded everything he had together in his briefcase and made a decision that he'd let go of the curious streak that had drawn him back into this mucky business. It wasn't as if he didn't have other work to do.

Thirty-Eight

Despite the promise he had made to himself, Alec found himself drawn back into Rob Beresford country almost by chance, and once issuing its challenge, he could not but take it up

It had been a busy day. A break-in at the local supermarket which looked like the latest in a series of such crimes. The third dead cat in a month on the Campbell Estate where, it appeared, there was a growing fashion for shooting felines with air guns. A painful and difficult interview with the mother of a rape victim, a girl attacked so viciously she had spent three weeks in intensive care. It was clear that the girl could identify her attacker but was too afraid to do so. Alec had the job of telling the family that they had enough evidence to bring a police prosecution and, whether their daughter wanted it or not, she might well be called upon to give evidence in court.

Two in the afternoon found him within a street or so of where Clara had grown up and where her mother still lived. Alec hadn't really known what to expect when he knocked on the door of Mrs Beresford senior, but the woman who opened it didn't match any of the vague conceptions he had formed from Clara's description.

Her hair was short, greying, and, Alec suspected, coloured, though skilfully enough not to conceal but rather to enhance the grey. Dressed in jeans and a pale pink cardigan over a lighter shirt, she looked comfortable, neat, at ease. In fact, Alec thought, she looked very like her daughter must have been before grief bit hard at her features and creased them before their time.

Alec introduced himself and showed his identification.

'Oh,' she said. 'Is this about Robert?'

'It is, yes.'

'Then you'd better come in.'

She showed him through to a lavender room. The décor a little overbearing for Alec's taste. He liked lavender, but not on every surface. He declined the offer of tea. He'd drunk it by the bucketload in the course of the morning and felt as though his body was sloshing.

'What can I do for you? I've tried to call Clara but she doesn't say much when I do get through. Mostly it's that machine telling me to leave a message and I hate the damn things.'

'They have their uses,' Alec smiled. 'My pet hate is voice mail. I'm sure people just leave it on regardless of whether they're there or not.'

She smiled but looked confused and he guessed he'd lost her on the technical front.

'I came to ask you if Rob ever visited,' he said.

'Did Clara send you?'

'No one sends me anywhere apart from my boss,' Alec told her. 'Clara is convinced Rob never came, but Rob was bound to wonder about you.'

She nodded. Sighed. 'Yes, Rob came,' she said. 'Once he was old enough to make the trip across town. I guess he must have been fourteen or so the first time. Perhaps a little younger. It wasn't a regular thing, he'd just appear out of the blue from time to time.'

'And did you enjoy his visits?'

'He was still my grandson. So like his mother.'

She had avoided his question, Alec noted. 'And you got on well with him?'

'Yes, we got on well enough though, as I said, it would be occasional visits just out of the blue. I know his mother didn't know and that worried me, but if I'd phoned to let her know, I don't suppose she'd have thanked me.'

'And on these visits, what did the two of you talk about?'

'Oh, this and that. How he was getting on at school. Sometimes he'd tell me about Clara. He was very proud of her, coping on her own.' She pursed her lips as though that

184

left a bad taste. 'I didn't know him well enough to discuss much else. Sometimes, I used to wonder why he came at all.'

'Did he ever talk about his father?'

The lips pursed and tightened once again. 'He asked me,' she said frostily. 'Natural I suppose that a boy should be curious about his origins.'

'And did you tell him anything?'

'No. That was for Clara to do. Besides, I don't think she knew.'

That still rankled, Alec realized, even after all this time. 'But were names mentioned? Aiden Ryan. James Scott?'

She flinched and he knew he had hit home.

'They may have come up in conversation, yes. But I told him nothing. That,' she repeated pointedly, 'was for Clara to do.'

She got up, indicating that the interview was at an end; he'd had his allotted time and now it was done he should go quickly. Alec leaned forward in his seat but didn't stand. 'You must miss him, though,' he said. 'Even though the visits were few and far between.'

Clara Beresford's mother regarded him with cold dead eyes. 'He was dead to me long ago,' she said. 'Those visits were like brief appointments with a ghost. With the past. To be truthful, I was glad when he stopped coming.'

'And when was that?'

'About a year or more ago.'

'Do you know why?'

She shifted restlessly, awkward standing while he continued to sit. 'I assumed his mother found out. Other than that, I wouldn't know.'

'All right, Mrs Beresford.' Alec decided to let her off the hook. He stood and dug into his pocket for a card. 'If you remember anything more about your conversations with your grandson, please let me know.'

She made no move to take the card so he placed it on the arm of the lilac chair.

Thirty-Nine

Clara had closed the curtains and shut out the world. The world seemed especially unkind today. First Alec with his blasted list – he meant well, she knew, but she was beginning to wish he would go away. Then not a half hour after he'd gone a couple of officers in uniform. A rather serious looking man who described himself as Sergeant Brodie and a young woman who was introduced as Constable Wyatt.

A complaint had been made against her. A complaint!

The toad, it seemed had made good on his promise to accuse her of assault. Clara hadn't known whether to laugh in their faces or burst into tears. Fortunately, she'd managed to refrain from either and they had outlined the possible charges made against her and taken a formal statement.

Truthfully, there wasn't much Clara could argue with. She had thrown coffee over him and had followed the liquid with the mug, though that had missed and just bounced off the chair. It had broken when it hit the coffee table not the toad.

Clara, in her own defence, had explained the circumstances. Brodie just continued to look serious and dour. The woman, Wyatt, had made what Clara supposed were soothing and sympathetic noises, though to Clara's rather jaundiced ears, the clucks and coos belonged in a kindergarten not in her kitchen.

Well, Clara thought, if he wants his day in court, I shall be happy to oblige and they can say what they like about me. No doubt it'll be like mother like son. Violent and impulsive.

She flopped into her chair preparing for an evening staring at the television. She didn't have a clue what might be on and, frankly, she didn't care. It was not real – unless she happened on news or a documentary and, should that misfortune arise, she'd simply flip the channel. Clara, these days, just wanted the not real.

The sound of a car being driven rather too fast in the quiet road attracted her attention. 'Silly buggers, with all the parked cars this time of night.' She heard it screech to a halt outside her door.

And then the crash, the sound of shattering glass. The living room curtains belled inward for an instant and then the missile, trapped and cushioned by the layers of thick, soft fabric, thumped on to the floor.

'Oh!'

Clara got up and stared. Dimly, she was aware of a second screech of tyres as the car sped away. She stared at the object that had landed on her carpet. A brick. A flaming house brick. Someone had thrown a brick through her front room window.

Clara could hardly believe it. She'd half expected some violent reaction when and if people had realized what Rob had done, but, to her face at least, she'd had nothing but sympathy from her neighbours. Had this happened when . . . she might have understood. But weeks had passed.

Belatedly, she ran to the window and pulled the curtain aside, peered out into the street. The car had gone. Of course it had. She'd heard it go.

'Clara, Clara are you all right? Oh what a dreadful thing.'

Her neighbour and her neighbour's husband stood on the front lawn waving a torch about. Clara stared at them in stupefied surprise.

'Someone threw a brick,' she told them. 'It's here. It landed on my floor.'

Alec arrived to find the beat officer already there and taking Clara's second statement of the day. SOCO had been called, but it might be a while. The offending brick still lay where it had landed and glass sparkled against the blue of the carpet.

'The curtains absorbed most of it,' Alec said. 'It's lucky they were closed.'

'I always close them as soon as it gets dark.'

Alec nodded and got on the radio to see if he could hurry

things along with SOCO and make sure an emergency glazier could be found from the list they had at the station.

The beat officer came and found him in the hall. 'Not been a good day for her,' he said.

'Oh, more than this then?'

'It's in the day book. She had a visit this morning relating to an assault.'

'Ah. Assault with coffee mug.'

'The, er, victim made a formal complaint. I took his statement as it happens.'

'Lucky you. What's the betting the two incidents are related?'

'I'll lay odds.'

'So would I. If you've finished, you get off. I'll take it from here.'

He returned to Clara's kitchen. 'We should have someone round to collect the brick in under an hour,' he said, 'and a glazier in about two. I could get it boarded up for tonight if you'd rather. Late callouts do cost.'

Clara shook her head. 'It'll have to go on the credit card,' she said. 'Bastards. You know it was the toad, don't you?'

'No. I don't know. You only suspect.'

'Right, ever the sceptic. You know what that . . . did?'

'I've just been informed. Clara, I'm sorry.'

'Nothing you can do. I threw the mug. I just . . . I wish it had been hot, that's all. Burned the bugger.'

'It wasn't then?'

'Not really, no. I'd drunk half of it. Not that it matters, I suppose. The intent was there.'

'There is that. Clara, I hate to add to your troubles, but I saw your mother today.'

'My mother? What the hell for?'

'I wanted to know for certain whether or not Rob had made contact with her.'

'Christ, you expect her to tell you the truth?'

'Why would she lie about it? Look, I know how you feel, but Rob did go, several times in fact. He knew about Aiden Ryan and about James Scott long before we thought he did.'

'I don't understand.'

'According to your mother he stopped coming when he was about sixteen. She thought you must have found out and put a stop.'

'I'd no idea.'

'But she more or less admitted that their names had come up in conversation during one of his visits. It wasn't finding Aiden's picture that set him off the month or so before he died. It was something else. It's perfectly possible he didn't find the Ryans until recently, but Aiden was certainly on his list from some time ago.'

'But James Scott. There was nothing on his computer.'

'Not that we've found so far. He may have kept other records.'

'She told him. She went behind my back and she told him.'

'He went behind yours and asked her,' Alec pointed out.

'That bitch.' Clara wasn't listening.

'You're sure James Scott didn't mention a meeting, not when he came over?'

'I'd have remembered that. Damn right.'

Alec nodded. 'OK,' he said. 'I'll be speaking to Mr Scott in the next day or so, about Rob and about a certain brick. I'll see what he knows.'

She nodded weakly. 'It just gets worse, doesn't it?'

Patrick had done his best to keep the conversation neutral. He wasn't sure it was always a good idea to talk about the same thing over and over again, especially when it was so clearly personal. Jennifer, it seemed, had rowed with her mother again, this time about the name of the baby. Her mother had asked if it was a boy that Adam should be included in the name somewhere. Jennifer didn't want it. She was, at least, sensible enough to understand she couldn't get away with naming it Robert, but she was still trying to get as close as possible.

Did he have a second name
Who? Rob. I don't know.
You must know you were his friend
It never came up in conversation

189

Find out for me

I'll try but anyway, what if it's a girl

I'm sure it's a boy. I told them at the scan I didn't want to know but I wishes id asked now.

Patrick sighed. His machine chimed and Charlie popped up in a second box. He'd changed his signifier again. Lyrics from something or other, Patrick guessed. Charlie was a fan of seventies rock and his designators usually reflected that. Last week he had been, simply, Marc Bolan. Now he was something about black dogs.

Hi, hows things

OK. Done your essay yet.

Did it already so I didn't need the extension.

Well get you.

Jennifers on. She's driving me mad. Can I invite her to chat?

I don't know about that.

Please Charlie. I like her but she's so intense I don't know what to say to her most of the time.

Shouldn't have got involved. OK, if we must.

Thanks Charlie.

Relieved, Patrick relayed Charlie's invitation to Jennifer. The result was not quite what he had expected.

Bored with me are you? Want to talk to someone else? Patrick youre the only person ive got to talk to right now surely you can spare me a bit of your precious time.

Don't be like that. Charlie's OK. Well have a laff.

Maybe I don't feel like laughing.

Maybe it would do you good if you did.

Across the network, Patrick could almost feel the frozen silence.

I think I ought to go now and leave you to talk to your friend.

That wasn't what I meant.

Patrick hated people who tried to manipulate him this way. Irritated, he fired back. *OK, if that's the way you feel goodnight then.*

He waited, but she made no reply. A minute later she was gone. Patrick sighed.

Why don't you block her, Charlie asked

Don't know. I'm thinking about it. I just wanted to be friendly but she acts like she tried to own me.

Wonder if she was that way with Rob

Don't know, Patrick replied. *But its driving me nuts.*

Becks still isn't back at school. I thought id just missed her but she wasn't in. I phoned her house and her mam says she's sick and doesn't want to talk to anyone.

Great. Its not my fault Charlie but I feel bad about it.

Not your fault. She'll get over it.

You think so.

He'd not told Charlie about the list. Charlie had assumed Patrick had backed off from the search. Alec had promised that if anyone should ask, he'd say it was someone on the force that got the information. That's the way it should have been anyway. Patrick was glad and annoyed at the same time. After all, he'd done a good job, finding out. But, if it was a matter of taking credit or losing Becks and Charlie it was a no brainer. His friends mattered more.

OK, Charlie wrote. **Some of us haven't been little goody two shoes and finished our work early so I must be off. Just wanted to check you were ok.**

Thanks. See you t'morrer.

He signed out completely and stared at the screen. Jennifer seemed to be picking fights with all and sundry. He knew pregnant women were often moody, but she did seem to be making a meal of it. Still, he thought, I suppose she's got a lot to be upset about.

He wondered about the pictures she'd avoided telling him about. Hinting so he'd ask for more, not realizing that Patrick didn't play that game.

Pictures Adam Hensel had taken. They had to be of her and they had to be . . . well, not the sort you put in a family album.

Forty

James Scott was not at work. He was ill, apparently, though Alec could see no sign of it. Scott's wife let Alec in, and then went back upstairs. Alec heard the Hoover fire up and suck against the floor above.

'You've come about my assault, I suppose.' James said. He was squashed into a reclining chair, a mug of tea in his hand. Alec could see no trace of anything on his face, particularly not hot coffee burns.

'No,' he said. 'Actually, I came about a brick.'

'A brick.'

'Yes. It was thrown through Clara Beresford's window last night at around eight fifteen. Witnesses saw a car drive off at speed and we have a partial number. Then there's the brick, of course.'

'Why should I be interested in a brick?'

'Well, if you had nothing to do with the throwing of it, then you don't need to be interested, I suppose.'

'She assaulted me. Why should I care anyway if someone threw a brick through her window? I go along, offering sympathy and she chucks a mug of scalding coffee in my face.'

Alec studied James Scott's face. He got up to take a closer look and made a big thing of examining him from all angles.

'You must heal quickly,' he said.

'I had it photographed. Red, I was, like a lobster.'

'Hmm. Did Robert Beresford ever visit you?'

'Visit me?'

'Well, you might have been his father. Maybe he came to see what you looked like.'

James Scott scowled at Alec. 'What makes you think I'd have welcomed him if he had?'

192

'Well, you did go and see Clara Beresford, assure her of your continued interest.'

'My continued what?' The Hoover fell silent and both men looked up. 'Now listen, I don't want any trouble.'

'No? Does your wife know who you're accusing of assault?'

'She knows, yes. Clara Beresford owes me. Compensation, that's what I want from her. I've been off work since it happened. Shock and stress and mental anguish she owes me for as well as the damage she did to me face.'

'Really. So Rob didn't visit you?'

'You sound like a cracked record. How the hell would I know?'

'Well, he might have knocked on the door and said "hello dad".'

Jamie Scott lifted his eyes heavenward again, but Alec didn't think he was appealing to the Almighty.

'He might have done,' he conceded. 'But he were a cheeky little bugger and I sent him on the way. He only turned up the once.'

'Didn't show you the respect you deserved, then,' Alec asked.

'No, he bloody didn't.'

'Think you were a bad catch on the paternal front, did he?'

'You what?'

'Never mind. Now. About this brick.'

'That again.'

'Yes that again. It won't be long, you know, before we can get a handle on who threw it. Then it's just a matter of matching samples.'

'Samples?'

'Yes. DNA, you know. Whoever handled the brick . . . perfect surface for collecting DNA it being a rough surface and all.'

'He might have worn gloves.'

'Might have, but didn't. We've got samples for analysis, Mr Scott. I expect someone will be round in the next day or so, to ask you for a little of your DNA for analysis too. For elimination purposes, you understand, you being known to be in conflict with the victim.'

'I'm the bloody victim.'

'Not of assault by brick,' Alec said.

He took his leave shortly thereafter, meeting Mrs Scott in the hall on the way out. She was standing with her arms folded across her chest and did no more than nod when he said goodbye.

Alec wondered how much she had heard. He hoped it had been plenty.

Driving away, he couldn't help but wonder how a woman like Clara could have gone out with a man like that. Though, to be fair, they'd both been little more than kids at the time and James Scott may have been much more of a catch. What, he wondered, was the present Mrs Scott's excuse?

He wondered too how long it would be before James Scott dropped charges against Clara. He'd enjoyed himself. He had no idea whether or not there would be DNA on the brick and if there was and it was analyzed it wouldn't be on the fast track at the lab. But James Scott wouldn't know that. Alec hoped that at the very least it would give him a sleepless night.

Jennifer was waiting for Patrick when he came out of college. She'd been standing on the corner about twenty yards from the college which gave her a good view of the entrance.

She'd almost given up on him, the main river of students having flooded from the school on the stroke of quarter past, but Patrick didn't appear until the full half hour.

Her heart sank. He was with Charlie and that girl, Rob's so-called girlfriend. She watched with relief as they parted at the gate and went off the other way.

'Patrick.'

Deep in thought he'd not noticed her. He looked shocked. 'What are you doing here?'

'I came to see you.'

'Why?'

He looked cross, irritated and Jennifer began to think that this had been a mistake.

'To apologize, I suppose. I behaved like a moron last night.'

'Yes,' he said. 'You did. I was trying to help.'

'I know.' He moved on and she fell into step beside him. 'Walk me to the bus stop? It's on the promenade.'

He hesitated and then nodded. 'OK.'

They walked in silence for a few minutes. God, Jennifer thought, this isn't going the way I wanted. She tried to find an opening, a way of getting to what she wanted to say, but none seemed obvious. Finally, she just went for it.

'Have you ever done something you're ashamed of?'

He glanced sidelong at her. 'I suppose. Everyone must have some time or other. Why?'

'I let him take pictures of me.'

'Who? Rob?'

'No. Like I told you the other night. Uncle Adam. God, you must think I'm a right slapper.'

'No, why would I.'

'You must do. I told you about Adam's pictures and then you asked if I let Rob take them too and anyway, look at me. Pregnant and it wasn't even a boyfriend.'

'You told me there were pictures,' Patrick pointed out. 'You didn't actually tell me they were of you.' He seemed to hesitate and then he asked bluntly. 'Was it your uncle?'

Momentarily shocked she halted and stared at him, then shook her head. 'No, I'm pretty sure it wasn't. I wanted . . . that night when he took the pictures we'd been flirting and mucking about and I'd got a bit drunk and I was messing about on his computer and I'd found these photographs of this woman and I thought . . . or rather I didn't think . . . you know. If that's what he wants, well, so I handed him the camera and I started posing, with my clothes on and then I started to get undressed and at first he got all, you know, get dressed again and I should take you home, but I told him he couldn't drive because he'd been drinking and anyway . . . he took the pictures of me. I woke up the morning after and I wasn't sure, you now, if we'd . . . if it'd gone further than that.'

'Did you tell Rob?'

'Yeah, I told Rob. He was all, you know, have it out with

him. But I know Uncle Adam didn't get me pregnant. I never stayed in his flat again after that night and that was in August so . . .'

'Who was it then?' Patrick asked directly. 'Was it a one night stand sort of thing? Clara said that's what happened with . . .' He stopped as though belatedly realizing he was talking about Rob's mum and her dad. He remembered too that Clara had more or less discounted Aiden.

'Yeah, I know,' she said. 'Yeah, it was pretty much like that. I was at this party and there were these two boys there and I got talking and drinking and one thing led to another and I'd had a row with my mum so I guess I wasn't . . . I guess I wasn't as in my head as I should have been and anyway these two boys, I sneaked out the back with one of them and we did it. Next thing I know I'm pregnant and I don't even know his name.

'Anyway, like I'm going to land him in it just because of one night'

'Didn't he use anything?'

She rolled her eyes like one of her favourite emoticons. 'I was meant to be on the pill. Mum doesn't know and it's the mini pill and sometimes I forgot to take it. I forgot to take it more often that I remembered, I suppose. By the time I'd figured out what was going on it was too late for the morning after pill and I didn't feel right about killing it. Not its fault its mum's stupid, is it?'

Patrick was the first person she'd said any of this to. She watched his face in the yellow light of the street lamps as this dawned on him and wondered what he'd do with the knowledge. Part of her wanted him to tell. Tell someone, anyone, save her the difficulty. Part of her was terrified he would.

Patrick's next question showed her he'd worked out something else as well. 'You let Rob believe it was Adam, didn't you?'

'I didn't *let* Rob think anything. He made up his own mind. I think he was going to talk to Adam no matter what I said, but, Patrick, I didn't even know he'd been in contact with Uncle Adam, never mind arrange that stupid meeting. Then, they were both dead.'

'How do you know Rob arranged the meeting?' Patrick asked.

'I don't but he must have done, mustn't he?'

She'd gone beyond tears, all cried out. She tucked her hands into the sleeves of her coat and stared miserably ahead into the gloom. They'd reached the bus stop now and she leaned against the wall, staring out to sea until the bus arrived and Patrick said goodbye.

There, she'd said it all now but telling her parents would be ten times as difficult again.

Forty-One

Patrick wandered back to Naomi's. It was later than usual and he arrived just as his dad pulled up in front of the flats.

'I got chatting,' he said. He didn't say who to.

They took a moment to explain to Naomi and then drove home, Patrick thinking hard about Jennifer and Rob and the whole conundrum. He found his thoughts were chasing themselves in circles, like dogs with too many tails. He could begin to appreciate how confused Rob must have been feeling and why he had seemed so moody and out of sorts in the weeks before his death. He wondered if Adam Hensel had felt the same. If he too had tried to make sense of something that, well, that just didn't.

What Patrick couldn't really get his head around was why Jennifer thought it better to let people think the father of her baby might be either her uncle or the boy who thought he was her half brother, than that it was the product of a stupid one night stand. OK, so that wasn't something she might want to shout from the rooftops, but it was a little less reprehensible, in Patrick's eyes, anyway, than was incest.

Was it still incest if it was your uncle?

He might not be the most popular kid in school, may not be invited to many of those sorts of parties, but that didn't mean he wasn't aware of them or aware of how much sex went on – along with how much booze. He had heard girls talking to one another about this boy or that and how they'd never . . . not at a party and then heard the boys in question boasting how they had. Actually, Patrick thought, sometimes it was the other way around and he knew this wasn't a new phenomena. He'd once – and yes, he was ashamed of it, sort of – eavesdropped on Naomi and Mari gossiping about Naomi and her sister and their teenage years. The conversation had involved a lot of semi-shocked giggling and exclamations of 'you never', but he had heard enough to know they were talking about an old flame of Naomi's and what she now wished she hadn't done.

At least he found it comprehensible that Jennifer should indulge in a quickie behind the shed in someone else's garden. What he found less comprehensible was that she would pose for her uncle to take pictures. Or she should then tell her uncle that the father of her unwanted baby might be the same person she was trying to introduce to the family as her half brother.

Had she told Adam that? Either of those things? She had admitted that she had let Rob believe that Adam was more than just a maternal uncle. Patrick wanted to know, desperately wanted to know, if she had played the game the other way.

'Dad, did you know Naomi when she was my age?'

'Well, yes. I've always known Naomi.'

'No, I mean as a close friend, like you are now.'

'No, we sort of drifted apart in our teenage years. I was the quiet sort, I suppose.'

'And Naomi wasn't.'

Harry chuckled. 'Oh no.' He sobered quickly. 'Why the questions?'

'Oh, I don't know. I'm not close to many girls. Becky, yes, but girls are . . .'

'It doesn't improve when they turn into women,' Harry said. 'I certainly never understood your mother. That's why she left me.'

Patrick laughed. 'You get on OK now though.'

'Oh yes, but we've got all that ocean between us and the only thing we really talk about is you. We've always been in agreement when it comes to what we feel about you. And, you know, I'm really glad you get on with her new family. Relations are a bit thin on the ground this side of the pond and I've always had this worry, you know, what might happen if I . . .'

'Oh, Dad.'

'What is it Naomi says? Part of a parent's brief to embarrass their offspring?' He pulled into the drive and Patrick got out and opened the front door. He dropped his bag in the hall, picked up the mail and went through to the kitchen.

'And is there a particular girl that's causing this grief?' Harry asked him, following him into the kitchen.

'Oh Dad, like I'd tell you.'

'No, I thought not. But I have to try. Another section of the parent charter. All I can say is, I'm glad you're not a girl. I don't think I could cope.'

Patrick smiled at his father. 'Well, at least I did something right. I got myself born the right sex.' Then he frowned and his expression darkened, closed. 'It's Jennifer,' he said. 'Adam Hensel's niece, you know. I met her at Clara's that night and I've been talking to her on MSN.'

Forty-Two

A lec was summoned to his boss's office as soon as he arrived that morning. A complaint had been made against him. One James Scott, accusing him of intimidation,

Chief Inspector Lyndon was a relative newcomer to Ingham and he had Alec's record open on the table in front of him. 'Not the first such accusation that's been made, is it?'

'No, nor do I expect it to be the last. I was acting on a hunch, sir.'

'A hunch. I don't suppose you checked the bloke's alibi before you stormed in on your hunch?'

'Alibi? I didn't accuse him. I asked. I made the suggestion that the brick through the window might have had something to do with him.'

'You told him he'd have to give a sample of his DNA.'

'Strictly for elimination purposes. Nothing more.'

Lyndon snapped the file closed and glared across the desk. 'Don't you think you're getting a bit involved with this Beresford business? Hardly the best use of police time, is it? Drop it, Alec. The case is closed, to all intents and purposes. Hensel is dead, so is the kid that did for him. Nothing more for us to do.'

'Apart from find out why.'

'You want to fund the overtime to do that? Fine. The resources of this department are stretched thin enough as it is without you skimming them out on things that don't matter.'

'Funny, I thought establishment of motive was a prime concern.'

'Don't play games, Alec. Motive matters when you're trying to find the perp. Not after the event. What's eating you, anyway?' he asked in a more conciliatory tone.

Alec sat down. Where to begin. 'I found a link between murderer and victim,' he said.

'So I believe. The boy thought the dead man's brother-in-law might be his dad.'

'It's likely Rob also thought the dead man got his niece pregnant.'

'And did he?'

'I don't know. He did take some rather compromising pictures. But she was over sixteen at the time and at least semi-consensual.'

'Semi?'

'Drunk.'

'Oh. Tell me something new. OK, so you have a possible motive. Rob Beresford taking revenge for uncle getting girl pregnant. That your angle?'

'That's part of it,' Alec said slowly.

'So, you have possible motive, end of story.'

Alec wondered if he should bother getting into what was found on the computer drive. 'Look,' he said. 'Give me some bodies, a couple of hours for house to house. We cover a narrow area, the cul de sac where the attack happened and say, a hundred yards each way up the main street. We turn up nothing new, I leave it at that.'

'Alec, you're talking like you're calling the shots.'

'I wouldn't presume.'

'Like hell you wouldn't. Christ, Alec . . . OK, you and three others. No more than two, three hours. I'm not calculating the cost. Make use of the Community Liaison bods and the Specials, I can't spare anyone on shift. Now get out of here.'

Alec grinned. 'Thanks,' he said. 'Oh, one more thing?'

'What now?'

'Did he have an alibi? Scott?'

'Only corroborated by about fifty witnesses. He was down the pub, performing on the flaming Karaoke.'

Patrick went straight to Naomi's after school and asked her if he could use MSN. He'd recently set up an account for her and taught her to use the message record function so she

202

could speak into it and he could talk back. She'd not really used it much yet, but the idea appealed as she could manage that with only a couple of key strokes. Patrick had put clear, textured sticking plaster on the relevant keys so she could find them.

Jennifer was already online. He'd started to think she must sign on the moment his school day finished and be waiting for him. He came straight to the point.

Did you make Adam belive that Rod was the dad?

Well hello to you too. What's all that about.

Straight question but I want an answer. Did you?

How should I know what he thought? I didn't make him think anything.

But you didn't tell him otherwise did you? Very clever wasn't it making Rob think it was Adam and Adam think it was Rob. Bet that made you feel really good having them both fighting over you.

What? Why are you doing this Patrick I thought you were my friend.

So did Rob. Look I want to know thats all.

Nothing came back from her for so long he thought she'd just logged off and that would be that, but eventually she typed:

Maybe they thought that I didn't know. It was easier in the end to let them think it and stop asking me stupid questions.

Why not just tell the truth.

The truth. Yeah great.

Patrick was confounded. The more he thought about it the more certain he was that her lie – no, it wasn't even a lie – her failure to tell the truth had led at least in part to this tragedy. He could imagine, both men, righteously angry; Adam carrying, perhaps, the added guilt that it *might* be his baby. Or might *have* been if things were different.

Did you know they were meeting that night?

No. of course not.

Patrick, getting used to Jennifer's interpretation of fact, rephrased. *Did you know they were planning a meeting any time?*

Rob might have hinted at it. He wanted to get things out in the open.

And if he had done, got things out in the open, then everyone would know you were leading them on and the father was someone else.

And what's that supposed to mean? That I wanted Rob to kill Adam? That I wanted Adam to kill Rob? Your mad you are. Nuts. A freak. Emoticons bounced across the screen, crying, shouting, mouthing at him as though she'd run out of words.

He had to think more, sort this out. Abruptly, he logged off and sat back in the chair staring at the screen.

'Trouble?' Naomi asked.

'No. Why?'

'Because you don't type that fast unless you're annoyed about something and don't care about the spelling.'

He scowled. 'Who says?'

'I do. Hey, look, if it's none of my business, tell me so.'

Silence.

'OK, I consider myself told.'

Patrick sighed. He didn't want to argue with Naomi or upset her but . . . he didn't think he could use the right words to explain either.

'Look,' he said. 'I'm sorry. Truth is I can't really tell you what it is because . . . right now, I don't really know.'

Alec's team had more enthusiasm that experience going for them, but he was happy to accept eager and try and instil a little finesse.

'These people have all given statements before,' he said. 'Then there's a list of those who saw nothing and a third list of people who were out when we did the house to house before and we haven't spoken to.'

The previous enquiry had been carried out in daytime and a brief follow up one evening, but Alec figured it would have been very easy to have missed the workers.

'Remember, we're jogging memories, not feeding people lines. And please people, unless it's very obvious someone does have something new, please stay on the doorstep. Once inside you'll be faced with every grievance from the past five years, from the neighbour parking their car in the wrong place to missing cats, and while I'm all for community policing, I've only borrowed you for a couple of hours. We hit nine o'clock and your line managers'll be screaming at me to give you back.'

His comments were greeted with laughter and knowing looks. Alec assigned tasks. The community liaison officers were given the 'didn't sees and the no shows'. Alec and the special constable, a long server by the name of Raymond Parks, split the rest, those who had actually made statements after some fashion or another.

Of these there were a scant half dozen, but Alec knew from experience that they were unlikely to get through more than that in the time allotted, especially if anything new should happen to arise. It was a job requiring time, experience and patience and right now, they were short on two out of three of the equation.

'Remember, maintain radio contact. Anything at all comes up, or anything you're not sure about, give me a shout and I'll be there.'

Nods all round. He was aware that they thought this was a wild goose chase, but it was something new and Alec's reputation meant that their being selected, even for the chasing of wild geese, made it something of an occasion.

Alec, frankly, was having second thoughts about the entire thing. It was raining, that cold stuff that can't quite make up its mind to be snow but which worked itself into every gap in clothing and found every millimetre of bare skin. He was tired, hungry and becoming convinced that his boss was right. It was sheer bloody mindedness that kept him tugging at this. No logic, no reason, no excuse at all.

He hoped, in a way, that they would reach the witching hour of nine and nothing new would have been discovered, no witness come forward to disturb the desert of information with their breath of doubt. Then he could go home, tell everyone concerned that he'd done his best and move on to the next event the job threw at him.

For the first hour it seemed this would be so. No one

205

remembered more than they had done in the days immediately following the murder and when he checked in with the liaison officers, only two had been struck off the list of no shows.

'OK,' Alec told them. 'Just carry on.'

He worked down the main road from the T junction at the end, back to the corner where Adam had died, calling just at those houses where the occupant had something to tell. Ray Parks came down to meet him from the other side. The woman three doors down from the murder site had the most to give, but it was old news.

'I saw a figure,' she told him as she'd told the officers before. 'Someone running back down the hill towards the junction. It was the shouting that made me look out. That poor man, I suppose and someone else.'

'You didn't hear what was said?'

'No, I'm sorry, no. We had the television on you see. It was only when the shouts got very loud we heard anything and then it was more like a scream, I suppose and someone, I swear someone shouting "No". Just no. But very loud.'

'A scream.' That was new. The copy of her statement he carried just said shouting. 'Are you sure?'

'Well, yes. I thought at first it was the fox. We have foxes round here, they make a good living out of raiding people's bins. Oh, the mess they leave. But they are pretty things, you know. Anyway,' she waved a hand at Alec. 'You don't want to know about the foxes. But I thought it was a fox at first, you know the way they cry out to one another, high pitched and really rather eerie. Then we heard the shout . . .'

Alec thanked her. 'And the figure . . .'

'No more than a dark shape running in the road. If he'd been on the path I might have made out more, but the figure just took off, down the middle of the road. Down towards town.' She hesitated. 'Can you tell me if you've caught him? The man who did this? We've all been so worried, you know. Some of the neighbours said it was a boy who killed himself after, but you know how rumours go.'

Alec found himself telling her nothing, just platitudes about keeping an open mind, but that the killer had been brought

206

to justice and she needn't worry any more. He realized he had contradicted himself, but she seemed satisfied and Alec went on his way before she could ask him anything else.

Then he got a shout on the radio. One of the no shows from before reported seeing someone running from the scene. They'd phoned in and reported it, but heard no more.

'Probably the same as number twenty-three,' Alec said, but he went along to the address he'd been given. It was further up the hill and past where Adam Hensel died.

That, Alec thought, didn't seem right.

The man standing on the doorstep introduced himself as Marvin Kayne. He worked odd hours, so it had been hard to catch him in.

'I phoned the police the very next day,' he said. 'I told them, I saw someone running away.'

'Can you tell me more?' Alec asked. 'What they looked like, which way they ran. Any idea of age?'

Marvin nodded. 'Young, I'd say, they dashed across between the parked cars over there and I think they had long hair. Dark coat.'

'Over there?' Alec pointed to where Marvin indicated.

'Yes, between the cars. There's always cars parked that side of the road. Then up the path that way.'

'You're sure?'

'Absolutely certain. I heard shouting and I looked out through my bedroom window to see what it was about. I can't see the corner from there, but then I saw this figure. It'd been standing over there, in the shadows so I didn't see it till it moved. Then it took off up the hill.'

Two figures, Alec thought. It had been worth the effort tonight. One person, that must have been Rob, run down the hill towards the town. The other, break out of the shadows and take off the other way.

Forty-Three

Alec, vindicated and pleased with himself and his ad hoc team, was presenting his new piece of information to his boss the following morning when he was told he had a visitor.

'He says his name's Patrick Jones and he seems very upset about something.'

'Wheel him in,' Lyndon said. 'Go on, I've done with you. You've proved your point so far as it goes.'

Alec let that slide. What the hell was Patrick doing here?

He picked the boy up from the front desk and signed him in, took him to find a quiet corner of the canteen.

'I've bunked off school,' Patrick said.

'I'd worked that one out.'

'My dad'll kill me.'

'Ground you, maybe,' Alec said. 'I don't think Harry will see this as a capital offence.'

Patrick didn't laugh. Patrick always laughed at his jokes, however bad. That was understood. This was a bad sign. 'What is it then?'

'Jennifer. I think she made it happen. I don't mean she meant to, but she made Adam think Rob was the dad and Rob thought the same about Adam and . . . it sounds stupid now. I've been worrying about it all night and now it sounds stupid. Alec, I think she knew they were meeting that night. I think she wanted them to.'

Slowly, hesitantly, Alec coaxed the story from him. The things he had asked her and what she had said. It was clear from his expression that he felt he was betraying a confidence, if not a friend, but the older, more established care for Rob had won out over this newer more fragile one.

208

Guiltily, he pulled some folded paper from his pocket and gave it to Alec.

'My computer's set to record the chat sessions,' he said. 'I did it because sometimes we talk about how to do homework and stuff and you know what I'm like about remembering.'

'Sure. It's OK, Patrick. This is the right thing to do.' Alec skimmed the pages, ignoring the bad spelling and rather dodgy grammar. It told him a lot, much he already knew or guessed, but from a very different point of view.

'Last night's one is missing,' Patrick said. 'I was on Naomi's machine. I couldn't wait until I got home. I had to ask her.'

Alec nodded. 'Look,' he said, 'I'll drive you back to school, clear it with your head teacher and then I'll explain to your dad.'

'Thanks.' He clearly didn't want to go, but Alec thought it was the best place for him right now. Lessons would at least occupy his mind.

Alec was known at the college and Eileen Mather's secretary greeted him with surprise. Then Patrick with some alarm. 'Is everything all right?'

'It will be,' Alec said. 'But if Eileen's free, I'd like a word.'

'Of course, but I'm sorry, Alec, you'll have to hang on for a few minutes. She's got a student and his parents in there.' She leaned forward confidentially. 'Another suspension. Third this month. She is not a happy lady.'

They waited in the outer office. After ten minutes or so a boy came out. His parents flanking him like an armed guard. Alec could almost see the shackles.

'Now that,' he said, 'looks more like a capital offence.'

Patrick shrugged. 'He's a w . . . well you know. Always in trouble. He's been warned but he keeps bringing a knife into school. Miss Mathers said any student doing that will get kicked out, but they never do. Just suspended.'

Alec was interested. He'd always thought Eileen Mathers ran a tight ship.

'How come?'

Patrick shrugged. 'Dad says it's to do with funding. The

sixth form keeps getting smaller and everyone keeps saying we'll lose it altogether and merge with somewhere or other. Dad reckons if she keeps them on until, I don't know, November or something, she gets to keep the funding for the whole year.'

'And how does Harry get to know so much?'

Patrick shrugged. 'Mum was a school governor for a bit.' He grinned suddenly transforming his rather hangdog look. 'She enjoyed it.'

Alec laughed. 'I never met your mum,' he said. 'Patrick, is there much of this going on? The knives, I mean.'

He shook his head. 'No, not really. Some kids see it as cool, you know, kind of macho. Stupid. I nearly got done once, though,' he confided. 'You know the little knife I use for putting a point on my pencils? I forgot it was in my coat pocket. I told my tutor, soon as I got in and she locked it up for me, but if I'd been found carrying it . . .'

'Any of your friends carry? I'm not asking you to name names. Just curious.'

Patrick shrugged. 'No, not in school. It's handy to have a pocket knife though. Dad has one on his key ring.'

'I know. Though I don't think his Swiss army rip-off would have much street-cred, do you?'

Patrick laughed a little more easily this time. 'No, not really. Though all it'd take is some rapper to have one in a video and they'd all be after them. Charlie's got a genuine one, though I've only ever seen him use it to open bottle caps.'

'That figures.'

'Rob's mum said he had a pocket knife but we never found it among his stuff.'

Patrick frowned. 'He lost it ages ago. Rob was always losing stuff, that was just Rob. Then he got another one. An old thing, said he'd found it somewhere, in a shed or something. Charlie thought that was funny. Clara doesn't have a shed.'

Alec's heart skipped a beat. 'What was it like?' he asked casually.

Patrick shrugged. 'Sort of old looking. Wood with a blade

210

that had been sharpened so it was shorter than where it fitted into and kind of thin. It used to get stuck in his pocket and the lining would kind of catch on the blade when he took it out. It dragged the blade open. He cut his fingers on it no end of times.' He squinted, trying to remember. 'It had letters on it, I think.'

'The head will see you now,' her secretary told them, calling through from the other room and they went through, Patrick looking hangdog and guilty again.

This changed so much, Alec thought. This and the fact that there had been two people running away.

Forty-Four

'We've got a lead on your brick,' he was told when he got back to the police station.

'Oh?' The desk sergeant sounded amused, he noted.

'I hear you paid our Mr Scott a visit.'

'Might have done. Why?'

'Because it looks as though you got the wrong Scott.'

Alec laughed. 'So which Scott should I have harassed?'

'You should have tried his missis.'

'You're kidding me.'

'I am surely not. Your little DNA crack got her worried. She came down the nick and confessed everything.'

Alec roared with laughter, glad of a lighter note in what was becoming a very grim day. 'Revenge for the assault on poor Jamie, I suppose.'

'Not a bit of it. She'd decided, apparently, that Jamie Scott and Clara Beresford must already be having an affair and that the coffee throwing lark was designed to throw her off the track. So, she thought, a brick through the window might slow things down a little.'

'How did she figure that one?' Alec decided he never would understand women.

'Who knows. You looking for logic?' He leaned over the counter and whispered, 'Unless, of course you want to go looking for the whys and wherefores of this one too.'

Alec flicked at his ear. 'Get out of it,' he said. 'Thorough job, that's me.'

He left the guffaws of the desk sergeant behind knowing he'd be the butt of that particular joke for weeks to come and went to phone Ernst Hensel.

'I need to talk to Jennifer,' he said. 'Ernst, I'm going to

have her brought in. I'm sorry, but she's now a material witness.'

'To what? Alec, what is this?'

'To the murder of your son,' Alec said softly. 'Ernst, I'm sorry, but everything now points that way.'

Briefly, he outlined the new evidence they had.

'But, this proves nothing,' Ernst protested. 'Much of it is hearsay.'

'Much of it was written down,' Alec said softly. 'By Jennifer herself.'

'She thought that boy was her friend. I thought you were mine.'

'Ernst, you and Clara, you said you wanted the truth, no matter what it cost.'

'And then I asked you to let things lie. I told you we had suffered enough.'

'I couldn't do that,' Alec said. 'It had gone too far.'

Ernst was silent for a moment and then he asked, 'Has this not cost us enough already? Must this go on? I will fight for her, Inspector Friedman. I will convince everyone that this is a lie. That the boy is lying. That your witness is mistaken. That this is not so.'

'And what happened to your truth at any price?' Alec asked him wearily.

'Sometimes,' Ernst told him coldly, 'the price of truth is just too high.'

I didn't know it was his when she gave it to me. I just needed something sharp to cut a bit of string and she had it in her pocket. Keep it, she said. It's just an old thing. Just an old thing and sometimes it caught in my pocket because the blade was too short and stuck out wrong. I'd pull it out and it would be open. Later I saw the initials carved on the wood and I wanted to give it back. That night, I just wanted to give it back. To get a fair hearing, to have him tell the truth. All of that.

Then we saw her standing there and I don't know who was more shocked and I think it was then we figured we'd been suckered and I tried to give him back the knife. His knife.

213

Forty-Five

'He lied to me, everyone lies to me. Uncle Adam said he'd delete the pictures and Rob said he loved me and now Patrick, pretending to be my friend and lying to me.'

Interview room three was the cleanest and most comfortable. Her mother close by, still and silent and too tightly controlled, and Ernst, careful not to catch Alec's eye, sat in the corner with the female officer assigned to the interview. Alec had recorded their presence on tape and begun to ask Jennifer what had happened that night.

So far he'd got nowhere. Jennifer was like a stuck record, totally obsessed with her role as victim. She had a point, Alec supposed, from her perspective, they had all lied.

'Jennifer. Did you lead your uncle to believe Rob Beresford fathered your baby?'

She shrugged. 'I never said so.'

'But you never told him otherwise? And did you also lead Rob to believe that Adam had seduced you, had a sexual relationship that led to the pregnancy?'

She shrugged again. 'They all lied,' she said again. 'All bloody lied.'

'Jennifer. I can understand that you're upset. You must be very angry, feel let down in a big way, but you have to take some responsibility too. Two men are dead, Jennifer.'

'Not because of her!' Ernst shouted. 'Not because of her.'

Alec turned pitying eyes on the old man. He had slumped forward in his chair and seemed on the point of utter collapse. 'For the benefit of the tape,' he said, 'Mr Hensel just shouted out. I am arranging for Mr Hensel to be brought some water.'

'Jennifer,' he went on, 'did you follow your uncle on the night he died?'

214

She was staring at her grandfather. 'Grandad? Grandad I'm so sorry. I didn't mean for any of this.'

'I know, my love, I know.' Ernst took the proffered water though he did not drink. He seemed to rally a little. 'And now, my love, we have come this far and there have, as you rightly say, been far too many lies. For me, Jennifer, tell the truth. Let us all know.'

Jennifer bit her lower lip so hard Alec thought she'd make it bleed. She turned wet eyes upon him and then began to speak, not stopping until she was through.

'I didn't know for sure he was going to see Rob, but I had this feeling and Rob had been behaving so funny with me, like he didn't like or trust me any more. And I really loved him, you know. I really do. Uncle Adam hadn't been the same since that night with the photos. It was like he didn't want to know me any more and I was scared he'd tell. I felt bad. Felt sick and when I found out I was pregnant, I just wanted him to tell me it would be all right, but he was just like everyone else. Wanting to know who it was, why had I been so stupid. Rob . . . I never told him it was Rob, but he saw me with him one day and he jumped to the conclusion that . . . that Rob was the one. And I let him. I let him think that Rob was a secret boyfriend and that his parents would go mad at him if they knew. And there was Rob, pushing me to tell my dad about him and saying he wanted to get a DNA test done to find out once and for all and that if he got the money, he and me, we could have one done and that would prove if we were brother and sister.

'He didn't have much money. He wanted to know if I could get any. I said I'd try. I asked Uncle Adam to lend me some but he wanted to know why. I said I'd tell everyone about the photos if he didn't and he got mad then. I . . . I guessed he hadn't deleted them.' She lifted her tear-soaked gaze once more to Alec's face. 'He enjoyed taking them that night. I know he did. He kept saying that I was an adult now and that I was beautiful and I liked it. I'm so sorry Mum, but that's the truth.

'I let Rob think that I'd got something going with Adam. It turned him on, kind of. I think they both liked it and at first it was like a game. I felt so ugly and frumpy and stupid and it was nice, getting the attention. Having them feel sorry for me. But then it got serious.'

'When did you give Rob the knife?'

She shrugged. 'I don't remember. One day, his lace broke on his trainers. He had a bit of string in his pocket and nothing to cut it with. I had Uncle Adam's knife. It had fallen out of his pocket one day when he came round and I'd kept it, stuffed it in my bag and more or less forgotten it was there. I liked to carry it though. It made me feel safer if I was out on my own. That night. He'd come round and I followed him.'

'The night he died?'

'Yeah. He didn't see me. Then I saw Rob come up the road and I knew I'd guessed right. They started to argue, about me, and as they argued I . . . I began to realize they'd find out the truth about me. That I'd let them think . . .'

'And the knife. Did you see the knife?'

She nodded. 'Suddenly he had the knife in his hand and was reaching out towards Uncle Adam.'

'Reaching out?'

She nodded.

'Miss Ryan is nodding. Jennifer, what happened next?'

'They were struggling. I didn't see. Then Uncle Adam was on the floor, kneeling on the floor and I screamed and they both looked at me.

'And then I ran away. I ran away.'

Ernst leaned forward, face buried in his hands. Beth stared at her child, her face ashen and eyes wide, disbelieving.

'He might not have died,' she whispered. 'If you'd called for help, he might not have died.'

That was a step too far. 'Mrs Ryan,' Alec said. 'The medics have agreed that even had they been on scene when it happened it would still have been beyond them.'

'But she could have tried.' Beth got to her feet. She swayed, emotion unbalancing her. 'I'm sorry,' she said, and stalked, stiff backed, from the room.

'Mum . . .' The child's cry. Alec wanted to reach across the table and tell her it would be all right.

The price of truth, he thought. Maybe Ernst was right and the price sometimes was too high.

Epilogue

There was something about the sea, Clara thought, that soothed the nerves. Maybe it was the susurration of waves dragging at pebbles or the slow churn of the waves, low, predictable and yet never quite the same.

'So, a little girl,' she said.

'Yes, a lovely child. She has her mother's eyes. A few weeks early, but healthy enough.'

Clara nodded. 'I'm glad for you,' she said. 'I really am.'

Time didn't heal, she thought, but it numbed the pain, just a little, though not always in a good way. It was more the numbness you felt if you'd put your hand into this turbulent North Sea water and kept it there until it chilled. March now and the world was moving on.

'How are things,' she asked. 'With Jennifer and her mother?'

'I hope for a thaw,' Ernst said. 'The baby may bring one, who knows. She is hard to resist.'

'And you and Jennifer?'

Ernst sighed. 'I think,' he said, 'it will always be like this. A wound that heals almost too fast on the surface. The skin looks unbroken, but beneath, blood flows and the flesh is raw. From time to time I feel I must prod and poke at it just to see if the pain is still as sharp. It is, but I hope, in time, the skin will thicken and the wound will drain and dry. And you, will your wound heal and dry?'

'No,' Clara said. 'I wish you well and I will let the skin grow, as you say, enough to hope that Jennifer grows and thrives and becomes a loving mother, but no, my wound won't drain and dry. Not for a long time. Perhaps not forever.'

'You are a brave woman, Clara Beresford.'

'No, I'm a broken one.'

Ernst nodded and she took his arm, walked slowly along the sea strand, letting the wind and the sea bring a moment's peace to a troubled mind.